SHAMELESS

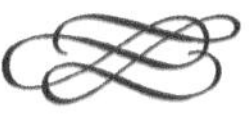

JENNIFER SUCEVIC

Shameless

Copyright© 2023 by Jennifer Sucevic

This is a work of fiction. Names, characters, businesses, palaces, events, locales, and incidents are either the products of the author's imagination or used in a fictitious manner. Any resemblance to actual persons, living or dead, or actual events is purely coincidental.

Cover Design by Mary Ruth Baloy at MR Creations

Evelyn Summers at Pinpoint Editing

Home | Jennifer Sucevic or www.jennifersucevic.com

Jennifer Sucevic Newsletter (subscribepage.com)

The Football Hotties Collection

The Girl Next Door

The Hockey Hotties Collection

MASON

I rap my knuckles against Derek Andrews' office door before poking my head inside the cramped space. "Hey, Coach. You got a minute?"

A bright smile flashes across his sun-weathered face as he pauses the game film he's watching and waves me in. "You don't need to knock, Mason. You work here now. Walk in any damn time you want."

The corners of my lips tug upward as I settle on the worn chair parked across from his desk. "That's gonna take a little time to get used to." As I glance around the office, my gaze slides over all the team photos that line the wall since he's been head coach for the Claremont Cougars.

That's fifteen years.

This is the man who recruited me when I was a junior in high school. I spent my freshman and sophomore years in college as his starting quarterback before my parents died in a boating accident. That day changed the course of my entire life. Instead of starting my junior year, I was forced to drop out and work full time as a mechanic to pay the bills and make sure my younger brother was taken care of.

Fast forward seven years and now I'm sitting in his office as an assistant coach. I have memories of him ripping me a new one when I'd fuck up on the field that are as fresh in my mind as the day they happened.

So, yeah…it's going to take time to get used to my new role as offensive coordinator for the Claremont Cougars. I'm thrilled about the opportunity but nervous just the same.

"Better wrap your head around it. We've got our first game in two weeks against Alabama. It's going to be a tough one. No two ways about it. What do you think about Levi? The kid has a solid arm. With the proper coaching, there's no doubt he'll continue to improve." He points a finger at me. "That's where you come in."

"He's talented," I agree. "From what I've seen, he needs to exert more control so he can send the ball to Ericson with consistency."

The older man nods. "Yup, that's exactly what I was thinking. You two will work well together."

When we lapse into silence, I shift and clear my throat. "I wanted to thank you again for giving me a chance to prove myself. I appreciate it."

His lips quirk as warmth fills his deep blue eyes. "I need a coach with your experience, and it's a great opportunity to finish up your degree. Especially with the break in tuition. As far as I'm concerned, it's a win-win situation."

My hand rises to the back of my neck to massage the area as I shake my head. "I've registered for a couple of classes," I admit reluctantly. "It's going to be weird going back after all this time. I feel so damn old around these kids."

He snorts. "What are you? Like, twenty-six?"

"Twenty-seven," I correct. "And now I'm a junior in college. Honestly, I didn't think I'd ever go back." After Mom and Dad died, it was the last thing on my mind. I was too damn busy taking care of my younger brother, Hunter.

"As long as you're employed by the university, tuition will be dirt cheap. There's no reason for you not to finish up your degree. It'll be just another tool in your toolbox. Certainly won't hurt you in the long run."

I jerk my shoulders.

Deep down, I know the older man is right. I need to take advantage of this opportunity. Especially when it'll cost me next to nothing. Since I'm now a full-time coach, I'll be spending most of my day on campus and my classes are a five-minute walk from the athletic center. It couldn't be more convenient.

And yet, knowing all this, I'm still riddled with second thoughts.

More like third and fourth thoughts.

Within minutes of registering for classes, I'd stared at my schedule for the fall semester and wanted to cancel all three. I know it doesn't make the least bit of sense, but I no longer feel like I fit in here. Not as a student. It's almost hard to remember a time when I walked around the gently rolling hills of this campus like I owned the place.

That's no longer the case.

"It's been seven years since I sat in a classroom," I add, just in case he's forgotten. "I'm not sure I remember how to study or take a test."

Even thinking about it makes the muscles in my belly clench.

Coach waves away my concerns as if swatting at flies. "You're stressing over nothing. I'm sure it's like riding a bike. Give it a week or two and then you'll be right back in the groove of things."

"I hope you're right," I mutter. Otherwise, it's going to be one hell of a long semester.

"I am. In a month, it'll be like you never left."

I huff out a breath, unable to imagine just such a scenario.

Not after all this time has elapsed.

Not after everything that's happened.

I'm three years away from turning thirty, for fuck's sake. Some of these kids are barely eighteen years old. They can't even legally drink. As soon as those thoughts pop into my brain, I shove them away.

It's tempting to drag a hand over my face.

When I remain silent, contemplating the merits of heading to the registrar's office straight from here and quietly withdrawing, he says, "There's no question that the last seven years have been rough. Now that Hunter has graduated and is playing in Atlanta, it's time for you to turn the focus back onto yourself. This is the perfect opportunity to figure out the rest of your life. Take advantage of it."

The man is right.

I know he is.

But that doesn't make it any easier.

Ever since Mom and Dad died, I've been operating strictly in survival mode, just trying to make it through each day and keep a roof over our heads. Now that my brother has graduated and is playing professional football, it should feel like a huge weight has been lifted from my shoulders. Like I can finally stand still and breathe again.

Strangely enough, it doesn't. It still feels like I'm on the cusp of drowning.

"By the way, how's Hunter doing?" he asks, interrupting the thoughts that churn through my brain.

My gaze flickers away and it takes effort to keep my voice neutral. "He's good."

A smile breaks out across his face. "That kid was one of the best players to come through this program."

I dip my head, silently acknowledging the sentiment. Hunter has always been a talented athlete. Even as a kid. Him turning pro was inevitable. And I did everything in my power to make sure that nothing derailed the plan. Whether my brother realizes it or not, I'd move heaven and hell for him.

"I'll let him know you said hello."

Although, I have no idea when that will be. The truth of the matter is that I don't talk to him very often. We've exchanged a few texts here and there since he graduated from Claremont, but not much else.

I did something I shouldn't have, and when he found out, it rocked our relationship to the very core. If there were a way to go back and make different decisions, I'd do it in a heartbeat.

But that's not possible.

All I can say is, at the time, I'd thought I was doing the right thing.

Turns out that wasn't the case.

Even though I've apologized dozens of times, he hasn't relented or forgiven me.

For the first five years, it was just the two of us clinging to one another. We were a unit. A team. It was the Price brothers against the world. Now that my relationship with Hunter is fractured, I'm on my own. The feeling of being lost and adrift has been my constant companion since he told me to go fuck myself.

To be clear, it was my fault.

I just wish he'd unbend enough to forgive me.

I stare down at my hands. I suppose that's one benefit to taking classes this semester—there'll be less time to dwell on the ways I've fucked up our relationship.

Hunter and Skye tied the knot right before her father died of cancer. Needless to say, I wasn't invited. That slight was like taking a cleaver to my heart. I never imagined there'd come a time when I wouldn't be invited to my brother's wedding.

"The three of us will have to grab a beer at some point."

That casually thrown out comment is like a fist wrapped around my heart, squeezing it until breath becomes impossible.

"Definitely," I force myself to say.

It's a relief when his phone rings, breaking the silence that has fallen over us and effectively ending our conversation. I shoot out of my seat like my ass is on fire and point to the frosted glass door. With a nod, he answers the call before swiveling in his chair and kicking his feet up onto a low bookshelf crammed full of beat-up binders.

A huff of relief escapes from me as I hightail it out of there.

POPPY

$\mathcal{I}$ tuck a stray lock of hair behind my ear and yank open the door to the men's locker room before stepping inside the space. Since the guys are on the field running drills, there's no chance of me walking in on a situation.

Been there, done that, and caught quite the eyeful.

It's only happened a couple of times, but the guys all grinned before hooting and hollering, calling my name with a wave. They don't seem to care in the least that they've been caught bare assed. A few of them actually seemed to enjoy strutting around and putting on a show.

Me, on the other hand?

My face turned about fifteen shades of red until it felt like I was in danger of self-combusting.

Talk about embarrassing.

The pungent stench of sweat and humidity hangs thick in the air as I walk past a long row of lockers and metal benches. When my phone buzzes, I fish it out of my messenger bag and glance at the screen.

A text from my roommate pops up. There's a bonfire at the beach tonight and she's already packing our bags, raring to go. Marissa enjoys partying with the best of them. She turns twenty-one next month and is in the middle of planning a huge bash. It's not that I don't like to drink or have fun, but sometimes, it's nice to stay home, order something in, and binge watch Netflix.

With my head bent, I turn the corner where the coaches' offices are located as my thumbs tap out—

I slam full force into what feels like a brick wall before reverberating off it. My phone is knocked from my hand before it skitters across the floor. Thrown off balance, a gasp escapes from me as I stumble back a couple of paces. Just as my arms pinwheel, strong fingers wrap around my biceps before yanking me forward. My breasts get crushed against the steely strength of a broad chest as I stare wide-eyed into the face of the man who now holds me captive.

For just a heartbeat or two, the world around me falls away and my mouth turns cottony as little electric pulses zip along my flesh. A million thoughts flutter through my brain, but they stall once they reach the tip of my tongue.

"Sorry," he says with a grunt.

We both come alive at the same time as he takes a quick step in retreat. Instead of releasing me, his fingers stay locked around my arms. The flesh beneath the firm grip feels like it's being singed, leaving permanent marks I'll carry around with me for the rest of my life.

I give my head a slight shake to clear it of the mental fog that has descended. It's not often I find myself at a loss for words. "It's fine. No worries."

When he rips his gaze from mine to glance at the floor, a sharp sense of loss slices through me.

"You dropped your phone," he says.

His voice is so deep and smooth that my belly does a little flip.

He relinquishes his hold before squatting down and grabbing the slim device from the tile. Once it's in his wide palm, he takes a moment to inspect it for damage. "Looks like you shattered your screen protector."

My attention stays riveted to the top of his dark head. It's so tempting to reach out and run my fingers through the thick strands. Instead, I tighten my hands into balls.

It takes effort to regain my bearings as I comb through my memories. Have I ever experienced this kind of visceral reaction to a man?

Nope. Never.

And that's another thing…even though I have no idea who this guy is, he's certainly not a boy. A thorough inspection of his face along with the fine lines bracketing his eyes suggests he's older, which means it's doubtful he's one of Dad's players. I dated one freshman year and vowed never to make the same mistake again.

So…if he's not on the team, who is he?

"Hey, sweetheart. What are you doing here?"

I jolt as my gaze swings from the dark-haired man to my father, who now fills the doorway of his office. It takes a moment to remember the reason I stopped by the athletic center in the first place.

"If you're not busy, I thought you might want to grab lunch."

The corners of Dad's lips quirk into an easy smile. "You know I'm never too busy for my girl."

The guy's eyes narrow as he rises to his full height, which is a couple inches taller than Dad.

Is that a flicker of shock-tinged anger filling his dark depths?

Interesting. It's there and gone before I can decipher what it means.

If anything.

Dad claps the younger man on the shoulder. "Mason, this is my daughter, Poppy. I'm not sure if you two have met before." He releases a chuckle. "If you did, it was a long time ago when Poppy was still in middle school."

Mason.

The name echoes throughout my brain before I commit it to memory.

His eyes widen slightly before resettling on me again. "I don't think so." Instead of reaching out to shake my hand, he gives me a terse chin lift. "Nice to meet you."

"Same."

"Poppy's a junior this year."

The other man nods. Whatever had flared to life in his eyes is now long gone. For all I know, it had never been there to begin with. I have no way to be sure. It all happened so fast.

Dad's face lights up. "Hey, why don't you join us for lunch. It'll give you two a chance to get to know one another."

Mason's gaze jerks from mine to my father before he shakes his head, not bothering to consider the invitation. "Sorry, I can't. I need to talk with the trainers about a couple players. Maybe another time?"

"Of course. Anne and I were just talking about having you over for dinner one of these nights. I'll check some dates and get back to you."

"Sounds good. Looking forward to it." With that, he takes a giant step in retreat. His gaze flickers to mine, touching on it briefly before looking away. "It was nice meeting you.

"Yeah. You, too."

Before I can come up with a reason to detain him, he swings away, disappearing around the corner. A couple seconds later, the locker room door opens before being slammed shut again, leaving Dad and I alone together.

"Do you remember Hunter Price?" Dad asks, recapturing my distracted attention.

Of course I do. If people were discussing Claremont football, they were talking about the talented quarterback. It was one and the same.

"Sure. Didn't he get drafted to Atlanta?"

"Yup," he says with a grin. "That was Mason, his brother."

Huh.

It's only when I conjure up a mental image of Hunter that I realize how similar the two men are. Both have dark hair and eyes, athletic builds, and are broad in the shoulders.

"Does he play professional football, too?" He certainly looks like he could, and from what I felt when I'd been crushed against him, he's all hard, sinewy strength. Desire flares to life in the pit of my belly.

Or maybe it flares a little bit lower than that.

Dad shakes his head before leaning against the door frame and crossing his arms against his chest. For a moment, his gaze drifts to the last place Mason had been before disappearing from sight.

"Nope. He attended Claremont and played for two years before dropping out. It's a real shame, because he was a talented quarterback. Since Jeff decided to take the head coach position at Wisconsin, I've asked Mason to come on as an assistant coach."

Interesting.

As tempting as it is to fire off a bazillion questions and do a deep dive on this guy, I keep them to myself.

For the time being.

"Where should we grab lunch?" he asks, interrupting the whirl of my thoughts.

"Poco Loco?" I say easily.

"Best Mexican in town."

I couldn't agree more.

And maybe—if I'm lucky—I'll be able to ferret out some information about Dad's new coach.

MASON

I yank open the door to the lecture hall and grind to a halt as my gaze coasts over the roomful of students laughing and chatting with one another. That's all it takes for uncertainty to crash over me again.

What the hell am I doing here?

I don't fit in.

Or belong.

I'm too damn old to be an undergrad.

I shift my backpack. The heavy weight resting against my shoulder feels more like a blast from the past than my current reality.

"Hey, you gonna move or what?" an impatient voice says from behind.

I blink and realize that I'm standing in the middle of the aisle near the door, holding up traffic. One glance over my shoulder shows a handful of annoyed people waiting to file into the spacious hall.

A dull heat creeps into my cheeks as I step aside.

"Sorry," I mutter, feeling even more like a dumbass.

It's so tempting to swing around and plow my way toward the exit. To forget about this idiotic idea of finishing up my degree and finally graduating.

What do I really need it for anyway?

Not the small mechanic business I started up a couple years ago out of my garage. That had been the plan before Derek Andrews filled my head with a bunch of crap about assisting him with his Division I football program.

I should have stuck with what I know.

What I'm used to.

Instead of giving in to every impulse that prods me to turn tail and run, I swing into the last row and slide over a couple of desks before settling on an empty seat. I promised myself I'd give this a couple weeks before dropping out, and that's what I intend to do.

No matter how painful.

Here's my dilemma—in order to coach college ball long term, I need a degree from a four-year institution. It took a lot of cajoling on Coach A's part to convince the athletic department to overlook that credential. They only agreed to hire me with the caveat that I take courses each semester and steadily work toward my bachelors.

If I quit school, I lose the offensive coordinator position. Not to mention, disappoint Coach, a man who has put his name and reputation on the line for me. Even though I've only been on the field with the kids for a couple of weeks, I already love it. This job is a dream come true. Now that I've made it a reality, I'm loath to walk away and go back to working on cars full time.

When I was a kid, I lived and breathed football. I played in a Pop Warner program before moving onto my high school team. And then Claremont. I have no idea if I could have played professionally after college, but I loved every moment of the experience along with the camaraderie I found with my teammates. The kind of friendships you make in a team sport aren't easily duplicated.

Until I walked away from football the summer before junior year of college, I didn't realize how much it consumed my life. I did the only thing I could and threw myself into steering my brother in the right direction. As satisfying as that had been, it's not the same as being on the field and playing.

Coaching isn't the same either, but it's damn close.

As close as I'll get.

So, no…the last thing I want is to give it up. Which basically means I need to do whatever I can to make the situation work. Since I haven't been in a classroom for a while, I decided to slowly dip my foot in the pond by taking a couple of classes. If the fall goes well… then I'll consider a full course load in the spring.

I still get my hands dirty by working on cars. It's just not as many as before. Coaching takes up a significant chunk of my time.

I glance around the room again and watch the other students grab their computers from their bags and fire them up. I can't help but shake my head. Back in my day, we used a notebook and pencil.

Isn't that easier than lugging around a laptop?

Just as that thought rolls through my head, feminine laughter catches my attention and I swing around and find the same girl I ran into yesterday outside Coach's office.

Poppy.

There hadn't been a doubt in my mind that she was young when I'd been staring down at her. But that hadn't been enough to stop me from yanking her close enough to feel the pebbled tips of her breasts pressed against my chest as her big blue eyes nearly swallowed me whole. It had taken every ounce of self-control to rip my gaze away.

Have I ever seen eyes such a bright and vibrant hue?

My initial response had been to drag her even closer.

Instead, I'd forced myself to do the appropriate thing and set her free.

A couple minutes later, Derek had stepped out of his office and introduced me to his daughter.

His daughter.

She's a junior like me…except much younger.

Seven years, to be exact.

What had he said while introducing us?

Right…that she'd been in middle school when I'd been in college. Even though it's been a couple of days, that comment is enough to make me cringe.

Obviously, she's way too young for me.

The girl is practically a baby, for fuck's sake.

Just like the rest of these damn kids.

But still…

My attention stays riveted to her as she flashes a grin. It's a little surprising when my cock twitches with interest.

When was the last time that happened?

Not recently.

The past seven years have been too busy. First, working at the garage in town and then branching off and starting my own business in the pole barn on our property. There's never been room for a woman.

All right, maybe that's not altogether true.

When I needed a warm body, I found one.

It wasn't difficult.

But a relationship?

Hard pass.

Even the most persistent of women tended to stop calling and messaging when they realized I had zero interest in being exclusive.

You want to spend a couple hours of no-strings attached sex between the sheets?

I'm your man.

Other than that?

Not so much.

When she laughs, I realize with a jolt that she's not alone. There's a guy at her side. One who's smiling down at her, staring like she's the only girl in the world.

My muscles tighten as my eyes narrow.

Wait a minute…I know him.

Levi.

The first string QB.

Tension fills every muscle.

What the hell is she doing with a football player?

Are they going out?

I'll tell you what…the way she'd stared up at me with those big blue eyes the other day had me thinking she was single. In fact, it had kind of felt like she might—

I shut down that line of thought before it can pick up traction inside my brain. It doesn't matter how she'd looked at me. Or what she'd been thinking.

Not only is she too young—barely out of her teens—but she's Derek's daughter.

His daughter.

Let that hard truth sink in for a moment.

Just as she's about to pass by my row, our gazes fasten and surprise flickers in hers. If I'd been trying to convince myself that they weren't as mesmerizing as I'd led myself to believe, that thought is blown clear out of the water.

They're even more stunning.

Electricity shoots straight to my dick. As much as I want to look away, I can't bring myself to break eye contact. It's only when she gives me a hesitant smile that I lift my chin in greeting before tearing my attention from her.

If I didn't know better, I'd say that the way my heart stutters before jackhammering a painful tattoo against my chest is a sign 0f things to come.

And not a good one.

POPPY

$\mathcal{P}$rofessor Lindstrom flips the page of the syllabus, going over every bullet point in pain-staking detail. I wish I could say I'm paying attention, hanging on every word, but that would be a lie.

I'm much too distracted by Mason Price, who's sprawled out a couple rows behind me. Every once in a while, I'll pretend to grab something from my messenger bag that sits on the thinly carpeted floor next to my desk. The excuse allows me to swivel just enough to glance in his direction and stare at the dark-haired guy who has been a constant presence in my thoughts since we ran into each other the other day.

God, he's good looking.

And I'm not the only one who thinks so. Most of the girls in his vicinity are turned in his direction, trying to catch his interest. It's a relief when he continues to stare straight ahead as if absorbed in the material.

Levi nudges my shoulder. "This is so freaking boring."

Knocked from my thoughts, I straighten on the seat and nod. "Yeah, it is."

"Want to grab something to eat after this?"

From the corner of my mouth, I whisper, "Sorry, can't. I have another class."

"Bummer. Maybe another time."

There's a moment of silence as Professor Lindstrom glares at the guy sitting next me. "Do you have a question, young man?"

When Levi clears his throat, I cringe.

This particular instructor is well known on campus for calling out wayward students who dare to talk during his lectures and shaming them into silence. From the rumors I've heard, more than one girl has run out in tears.

"Actually, I do. You mentioned a project that'll be due at the end of the semester." When the older man nods, Levi continues, voice growing more confident as he lounges on his chair. "I was wondering if we'll be able to pick our own partners or if they'll be assigned."

"They'll be assigned in a few weeks."

"Is there any way we can choose our own?"

A blush hits my cheeks as the professor's gaze flickers to me.

"No."

"Hmm. That kind of sucks."

"Yes, well, such is life," he says dismissively.

When Levi remains silent, the older man arches a brow. "May I continue, or do you have more questions?"

Levi's expression turns thoughtful before he nods like a king giving his consent for the festivities to continue. "You may."

The professor grits his teeth before shooting Levi one last glare. A few seconds later, he moves on to the next bullet point on what feels like a never-ending list. Unable to resist glancing at Mason, I twist in my chair again. Unlike the previous times, his attention is fastened to me. A burst of energy zips down my spine, making every fiber of my being feel as if it's coming alive. His jaw is tightly clenched as our gazes stay locked. Even from here, I can almost see the muscle ticking in his cheek.

It's only when Levi jostles me that I straighten. For the rest of the hour, I'm absurdly aware of the man sitting in the back. I can't help but shift on my chair with the need to twist around and see if he's staring or if the prickle at the nape of my neck is nothing more than my imagination.

Once the professor dismisses us, I shove everything inside my bag. Even though I tell myself it's because I need to hustle to my next class, deep down, I know that's a lie. It has nothing to do with the education course with my favorite professor and everything to do with my father's assistant coach.

When I scoot from the row, Levi glances at me with a frown. "Hey, aren't you going to wait?"

Instead of packing up, he's talking with a couple of teammates.

I shake my head. "Sorry, I need to get moving. But I'll catch you later, okay?"

Not bothering to wait for a response, I shimmy past into the aisle. My gaze darts to the desk Mason had been parked at, only to find it empty. I catch a flash of dark hair and brawny arms near the exit before he disappears into the corridor.

I huff out a breath. Unfortunately for me, the aisle is overflowing with people all moving in the same direction.

At this rate, I'll never catch up to him.

I almost falter as that thought flits through my head. Until this moment, I hadn't realized my intentions. Now that I have, I shove my way to the exit with purpose. A few students grumble as I cut them off. When I finally make it to the long stretch of hallway, I glance one way and then the other, but I don't see Mason anywhere.

Damn.

The disappointment that surges through me is almost shocking.

I race toward the main exit and push through the glass door into the sultry North Carolina heat. Even though it's only ten in the morning, I can already tell the day will be a scorcher.

I squint against the bright sunlight as my gaze scans the sea of students coming and going from the social science building. My heart stutters when I finally catch sight of Mason. Even though the walkway is congested, he sticks out with the broad set of his shoulders and thickly corded arms. Another round of arousal detonates in my core as I take off down the wide stone stairs and then the pathway to catch up with him. I hasten my steps, slipping through the pedestrian traffic.

A handful of seconds later, I pull alongside him. "Hey."

When he doesn't give me the time of day, I reach out and touch his bare forearm. "Mason."

Surprised by the contact, his gaze cuts to mine and goosebumps break out across my flesh. I'm just as bowled over by him now as I was the first time we ran into each other.

When he doesn't acknowledge the greeting, nerves explode inside me, and my heartbeat picks up tempo, pounding uncomfortably in my chest.

"Poppy," I whisper, attempting to jog his memory. "We met at my dad's office."

His gaze jerks away as he stares straight ahead. "I remember."

His voice is low and growly. It strums something deep inside me. It's as if there's an invisible thread tugging me in his direction. Pulling me closer. Reeling me in. The physical attraction coursing through me is almost too much for the confines of my own skin. Any moment, I'll burst at the seams.

"Oh." My mouth dries as I scramble for something to say. "I saw you in Psych class."

I glance away when his attention flicks to me for a second time, piercing the very heart of me. I've never had a problem talking to anyone before. But Mason is a different kind of animal than I'm used to. His penetrating stare makes me feel uncomfortable. Unsure of myself. Strangely enough, I have no desire to shy away or avoid him. If anything, I want to get closer and explore my reaction in more depth.

When we ran into each other last week and he wrapped his large hands around me, it felt as if the world fell away. The only thing I'd been cognizant of was the deep espresso hue of his eyes. Attraction and desire roared through my veins, filling all the dark spaces within. Ones I never knew existed.

It doesn't escape me that I'm like an idiotic schoolgirl with a crush. By the cool look in his eyes, my guess is that he agrees with the sentiment.

Ugh.

Heat slams into my cheeks. I was so intent on reaching him that it never occurred to me to come up with something to talk about. Maybe I should have, because the silence is brutal.

"I didn't realize you were a student here," I blurt.

"I'm part-time," he admits with a grunt.

"If you need any help with Psychology, just let me know." As soon as the comment shoots out of my mouth, I wish it were possible to shove it back inside. By the look on his face, the offer only seems to piss him off more.

This conversation is turning into a disaster.

"Poppy!"

Relief surges through me when my name is called over the din of students. We both turn to find Levi jogging toward us with a wide smile on his face. Just as he reaches my side, a thickly muscled arm is thrown around my shoulders. He hauls me close before glancing at Mason.

He blinks, his expression morphing into one of surprise. "Coach?"

A dull flush creeps into Mason's cheeks and the muscle in his jaw tics a mad rhythm. "Hey, Levi."

There's a pause, and I can almost see the gears in Levi's head turning, working in overtime. "Wait a minute...you're a student here?"

The disbelief that rings in his voice makes me cringe.

"Yup," the older guy bites out.

"Huh. That's cool." When he tugs me even closer, Mason's dark eyes narrow. "We just got out of Psychology. The professor was boring as hell. I'm gonna have a tough time staying awake in that class. What about you?"

"Same."

"No shit!" Silence follows that response before Levi clears his throat and drops his voice. "Sorry, Coach. I didn't mean to cuss."

"Don't worry about it." Mason shifts and glances away as if he's counting down the seconds until he can escape from us.

"Maybe we can all get together some time and study. Right, Poppy?"

Mason's gaze turns so frigid that a shiver of unease crawls down my spine and the muscles in my belly spasm painfully.

"Umm—"

"I don't think that'll be necessary" he interrupts, "but thanks."

"No problem, Coach," Levi says as if oblivious to the suffocating tension that has fallen over the three of us.

"I'll see you at practice." His gaze touches mine briefly. "Bye."

I lift my hand in a hesitant wave as he walks away, moving through the crowd with ease. People naturally make room, scampering out of his way.

"Sheesh. Someone's a grump in the morning," Levi mutters from beside me.

Not bothering to acknowledge the comment, my teeth sink into my lower lip as I stare at the older man's retreating form.

What's obvious from our stilted conversation is that Mason Price wants nothing to do with me.

MASON

$\mathcal{I}$ drag a hand through my hair before pressing the doorbell. When a couple seconds tick by, I shift and glance at the bottle in my other hand. The guy at the gas station wasn't any help when it came to picking out the wine. We both stood in the cramped aisle, staring at the limited selection before I finally decided that one at the midlevel price point was probably my best bet.

I don't know shit about wine.

What I know is beer.

Here's my advice when it comes to beverages with hops and barley —the colder, the better.

It's as simple as that.

The forced smile falters when the front door opens and I find Poppy standing on the other side of the threshold.

Well, shit.

It never occurred to me that she might be here for dinner. Is it too late to bail on this evening?

I'm thinking it is.

Plus, when your boss gives you a time to stop by for supper on a Friday night, you show up.

No ifs, ands, or buts.

"Hi," she says, hugging the edge of the door.

The hesitant smile simmering around the edges of her lips hits me square in the gut. It takes effort to force the air trapped in my lungs from my body. Every time we come into contact, my reaction to her is like a gut punch.

It needs to stop.

"Hey." Whether I want it to be or not, my tone is clipped and full of ice.

The fledgling convo stalls as we stare for a long stretch of silent moments.

Just as we nosedive into awkward, a hearty voice booms from within the house, "Good to see you, Mason." Derek glances at his daughter as he moves to stand beside her. "Poppy, let the man in. And look, he comes bearing alcohol."

Knocked from my stupor, a dull heat creeps into my cheeks as I shove the bottle into the older man's outstretched hand. "Hope this is all right. I wasn't sure what to buy."

Even though I try to keep my attention focused on Derek, I can't help but watch his daughter from the corner of my eye. She looks fucking amazing in a sundress that hits mid-thigh and hugs her curves. Since the first day of class, I've been doing my damnedest to avoid both her and Levi. I sneak in seconds before the lecture starts and find a spot in the last row before shooting out of my seat the moment Lindstrom dismisses us for the day.

That doesn't stop me from staring at the back of her blonde head throughout most of class. She's a distraction I don't need or want.

Coach leans toward me, and for a split-second, I wonder if he'll issue a warning to stay the hell away from his daughter.

I sure as hell wouldn't blame him for it.

"I'm gonna let you in on a little secret. Most of the time, Anne drinks it from a box. Upon occasion, a bag. The woman might have a fancy law degree, but she isn't overly picky when it comes to vino." He holds up the bottle. "This will be a real treat."

I don't realize air has become trapped in my lungs until it rushes from my body.

He waves a hand. "Come on, we're in the kitchen just putting the finishing touches on dinner. What can I get you to drink?" He glances over his shoulder and catches my gaze. "Beer good?"

"A beer would be great." It goes without saying that I'll need something alcoholic to get me through this evening.

As soon as I step inside the bright and spacious kitchen, a petite brunette flashes a warm smile in my direction.

"Mason," she moves around the long stretch of island before enveloping me in a hug, "it's so good to see you again. It's been way too long."

"You, too." As she wraps slender arms around me, my muscles tighten at the contact before I mentally force them to loosen.

When was the last time someone hugged me?

I can't even remember.

Actually, that's a lie. It was at my parents' funeral. That's what being embraced reminds me of—Mom and Dad's death. I've never been hugged so many times in my life as that day.

It's a bitter memory that stirs a painful ache in my chest.

The moment she releases me, I take a hasty step in retreat.

"Thanks for coming over. I'm glad we were able to find the time to get together." She gives me another smile. "Making plans during the season is always tricky."

"Thank you for the invite. I'm happy to be here." Well…I would be if a certain someone else wasn't present, driving me to distraction.

Coach claps me on the back. "I hope you brought your appetite along. Anne is an amazing cook."

A light blush hits her cheeks as she waves a hand before returning to the stove to check on dinner.

"Sure did." I clear my throat. "I don't get many homecooked meals, so I'm looking forward to it."

Anne glances over her shoulder with another easy smile. There's something calming about her presence. She has that innate power to make the people around her feel instantly welcome and comfortable.

"Spoken like a true bachelor. Feel free to join us anytime. I'm sure

Derek would love the opportunity to talk more football." Her eyes sparkle with humor.

"What?" Coach says, hand landing on his chest. "Me? No way. I never bring work home at the end of the day."

When the two of them chuckle, I force myself to do the same.

Yeah…there's no way in hell I plan on making this a regular event. Not if Poppy will be here. I don't like the way she makes me feel.

Nervous.

Edgy.

On constant alert…all the while being mildly turned-on.

I've only been in their house for a couple of minutes and already I'm having a difficult time keeping my eyes off her.

What is it about a pretty girl in a sundress with bare feet?

My cock stirs with interest.

Fuck.

I really need to do something to dampen the arousal rampaging through my body.

Our gazes collide and electricity sizzles through my veins as I force mine away and do my best to ignore her. My hand shakes as I bring the bottle to my lips and take a long swig, praying it'll douse the growing flames.

It doesn't.

Honestly, I'm not sure if anything can extinguish them.

This is exactly why I've been avoiding her.

Thirty minutes ago, I'd been looking forward to this evening. Now, I just want to make up an excuse and get the hell out of here.

As Poppy moves around the kitchen, helping Anne with dinner, the summery little dress brushes against her bare thighs. Every movement gives me another tantalizing glimpse of sun-kissed legs.

I take another pull from my beer as Coach talks about the new plays he wants the team to learn before our first home game. With a nod, I refocus my attention on the conversation. When he brings up our QB, I grit my teeth until my jaw begins to ache. I'm ashamed to admit that I ran his ass at the last practice. I think he's used to standing around like a prima donna.

You better believe I put a quick end to that.

By the expression on his face, the kid wasn't happy.

Unfortunately for him, there's more where that came from.

A hell of a lot more.

It's a relief when dinner is served on the deck. We all take our seats before digging into fish tacos, homemade yellow rice, and beans.

The first couple bites have my eyelids feathering shut.

Holy crap is this good.

Better than anything you'd find at a restaurant.

It's so damn delicious that I devour five tacos and have an extra helping of beans and rice. It's almost enough to make me forget that Poppy is seated in the chair next to mine.

Almost…

Every once in a while, she'll shift, and her dress will ride up her thigh. Even though I know I should look away, I can't bring myself to do it. My hand tightens into a tense ball so I won't reach out and trail a finger across her bare flesh. I bet it's silky soft. It's so damn tempting to find out. I want to stroke my fingertips from the delicate skin behind her knee all the way up to her

Nope.

I'm not going there.

The thoughts circle through my head like hungry sharks. The more I try to shut them down, the hungrier they grow until it feels like they'll gnaw their way out of my brain.

Every so often, she tries to strike up a conversation or ask me a question. I make it a point to answer in as few words as possible. If I could get away with grunting out a response, I'd do it. After about the fourth attempt, she gives up, allowing Derek and Anne to direct the conversation.

Now…if she'd just stop staring at me with those big blue eyes, I'd probably be able to make it through this dinner without losing it. I can practically feel her gaze licking over me. She doesn't even try to hide her interest.

Unfortunately, that turns me on even more than I already am.

It takes every ounce of willpower not to reach out and drag her onto my lap before taking her mouth in a punishing kiss.

Fuck.

Fuck.

Fuck.

By the time dinner ends, I'm a jittery, sweaty mess. I need to get the hell out of here before I self-combust. Anne and Poppy clear away the dishes while Coach discusses a few more ideas he's thinking about executing over the course of this season. I nod at all the appropriate intervals. Every time the voluptuous blonde walks by, I have to force myself not to stare.

It's not like I'm purposefully trying to be a dick. Although, I'm pretty sure that would be her assumption. The last thing I need is for her to think we're friends.

We're not.

And we aren't going to be.

She needs to understand that now so there aren't any hurt feelings or misunderstandings in the future. I can't be anywhere near this girl without the need to take her rushing through my veins.

So, yeah…it's better for both of us if I steer clear.

Just as I'm about to rise to my feet and tell them that I need to get moving, Anne brings out a key lime pie.

If I have one weakness, it's for homemade key lime pie.

Especially when it has just the right amount of tartness.

And this one does. Each forkful of the custard-like filling practically melts in my mouth. It's a little slice of heaven on a warm night.

Now that the sun has set, darkness floods the yard, and the stars brighten the velvety night sky. As tempting as it is to sit back and enjoy it, that's not possible. Not with Poppy in the vicinity.

I finish off my beer before setting it on the table and clearing my throat. "I should probably head out."

"Already?" Coach glances at the heavy silver watch wrapped around his wrist. "It's not even nine."

"Yeah, well…my boss scheduled an early morning practice, and I need to catch a few Z's so I can run their asses on the field."

"Sounds like the guy is a real jerk," he says with a chuckle. "But seriously, I'm glad you were able to make it for dinner. We'll have to do it again real soon."

"Definitely."

Not going to happen.

Once we reach the front door, Anne pulls me in for another hug and Coach claps me on the shoulder. I make sure to keep my distance from Poppy. She doesn't look surprised by my chin lift. But still, her attention never deviates from me. The muscles in my gut clench as her gaze slides over my body like a physical caress.

Before the evening can stretch any further, I hightail it from the house and to my old pickup parked along the curb. From the corner of my eye, I catch sight of a lime green Volkswagen Beetle in the driveway and shake my head in disgust.

It's such a girly car.

My guess is that it belongs to Poppy. I don't know her well, but it fits her personality to a T. Just go ahead and slap flower decals on the damn thing and call it a day.

Relief rushes through me as I slide onto the worn front seat and jam the key into the ignition. A second later, the engine roars to life and I pull away from the house, leaving it behind in the rearview mirror.

If only evicting Poppy from my brain were as easy.

Instead of heading home like I originally intended, I swing a right at the light and head to a little dive bar where the beer is cheap, the music is loud enough to blast the insistent thoughts from my head, and the women are easy. Maybe that's exactly what I need. Someone soft to sink inside of so I can forget about the girl with the pretty little sundress once and for all.

POPPY

*I*f there were any lingering doubts in my mind that Mason Price doesn't like me, they've been laid to rest this evening. He barely glanced at me the entire time he was here.

I made several attempts to draw him out of his shell by asking questions or making comments. His gaze would reluctantly flicker in my direction before he'd give me a clipped response. It was like I was talking to a Neanderthal who couldn't do anything more than grunt out his answers. After a while, I gave up. There's only so much teeth pulling I'm willing to do.

I have no idea what his problem is. My mind tumbles back to the other day. He must have taken offense when I offered my assistance. I was just trying to be friendly. All right...so maybe I was trying to come up with a way to spend time with him in order to figure out what it is I find so fascinating about the guy.

I hate to admit it, but the more he holds me at a distance, the more tempting it is to break through the roadblocks he's erected between us.

How's that for perverse?

"What a sweet man," Anne says, interrupting the whirl of my thoughts.

I blink back to the present and scrunch my face.

Sweet?

Did we have dinner with the same person?

There are several adjectives that come to mind when describing Mason Price, but sweet isn't one of them.

Moody.

Surly.

Standoffish.

Rude.

Those descriptors fit him to a T.

My stepmother raises a brow before studying my expression. "You didn't think so?"

I shake my head and fold my arms across my chest. "Nope. Not at all."

Her eyes cloud. "Well, I feel bad for him. I remember when his parents died. It was such a tragedy for the community but especially for those boys. Mason was just twenty and about to start his junior year of college. He ended up dropping out so he could get a full-time job to support himself and his younger brother. He was so proud and wouldn't accept help from anyone."

Part of me softens reluctantly. That is sad. And it gives me a tiny glimpse into why the man is so aloof. At least where I'm concerned. What's interesting is that when my parents were talking with him, I could see him visibly relax and lower his guard. It was those times when I sat quietly in the background, watching him while he was unaware. Whenever he flashed a smile at Anne or Dad, my tummy did a painful little flip.

"I think this coaching position will be good for him."

"Sounds like it," I say thoughtfully.

We chat for a few more minutes before I stifle a yawn. It's been a long week. "I should probably get going. Thank you for dinner."

Dad strolls out of his study, and I kiss them both before grabbing my purse and heading to the front door.

What I've learned tonight is that Mason has a lot of baggage. Instead of forcing myself on him, it would probably be best if I took a giant step back and gave him the space he's so desperate for. There are plenty of guys on campus who won't glare at me every time we make eye contact. I'll just have to find one who interests me.

And turns me on as much as he does.

Even though that shouldn't be a tall order to fill, it—unfortunately—is. I haven't had the best of luck when it comes to boys. Probably because that's exactly what they act like—*boys*. They want to party on the weekends and drink themselves into a stupor. Or play video games and hang out with their bros.

Unless they're looking to get laid.

Then, suddenly, you're high on their priority list.

No thanks.

Dad and Anne loiter at the front door as I slide behind the wheel of my Beetle and start up the engine. It sputters before roaring to life.

I roll down the window as my father jogs toward me and leans against the driver's side window. "That didn't sound good. We should probably get it checked out."

Since neither of us knows much about cars, I nod in agreement. It's been acting up for about a week, and I'm not sure if there's a problem.

"You want to stay here for the night? I hate the idea of you driving back alone."

I pat the steering wheel. "It's running now. I don't think it'll give me any problems."

"Text when you get home," Anne calls out from the front porch.

"I will," I say in a raised voice so she can hear.

With a wave, I back out of the driveway before stepping on the gas and speeding toward the entrance of the small subdivision. When I glance in the rearview mirror, Dad is standing in the driveway, shaking his head. I grin and turn up the music until the decibel level is a smidge below ear shattering as I turn onto the county road that leads back to town.

I'm midway through belting out a Billie Eilish song when the bug sputters and dies.

"What the hell?" My brows slam together as I steer the vehicle to the side of the road before slowly rolling to a stop.

Ugh.

For a moment, I contemplate the situation. It's not like there's much point to popping the hood and taking a peek underneath. Even if the problem had a flashing neon sign pointing it out, I still wouldn't know what I was staring at or how to fix it. Looks like Dad was right, and I should have stayed at their place. Instead of being stranded on the side of a county road, I could be curled up in my childhood bed, reading a good book.

Guess I'll call Dad and have him pick me up. We can deal with the car in the morning. With that thought in mind, I rummage around in my purse until my fingers lock around the slim device and pull it free. I hit the screen and wait for it to light up.

When it remains black, I realize it's dead.

Well, shit.

The battery had been low when I arrived at the house earlier this evening. I'd planned to charge it but got distracted by the guy who wants absolutely nothing to do with me.

Great.

Could this night get any worse?

I glance around the surrounding darkness. There are a few flickers of light in the distance amid the farmland and trees that dot the landscape.

Now what am I going to do?

Walk to my parents' house?

Sleep in the car until morning?

Neither of those options feels particularly safe or comfortable.

I force myself to step out of the Beetle before staring at the long ribbon of road. I'm about three miles from my parents' house. I glance in the direction I was heading. It's probably two miles to the edge of town and then another two to my apartment near campus.

With a huff, I decide that walking back the way I came makes the most sense. Since it's late August, the days are still in the high eighties and the nights usually drop to the mid-sixties. I run my hands over my bare arms, wishing I'd been smart enough to bring a sweater. I look at my choice of footwear. The sandals are super cute and totally go with the dress but won't hold up to a three-mile walk. By the end of my trek, I'll no doubt have blisters.

But still…what other choice is there?

Since the window is rolled down, I lean against the driver's side door and reach for my bag on the passenger seat. Just as I straighten, bright headlights fall on me. Raising a hand to my eyes, I squint against the harsh glare as the vehicle slows, rolling to a stop behind my car. My heartbeat picks up its tempo, thundering harshly against my ribcage as I toss the purse back inside.

It's only when the driver's side door opens and someone steps out that I realize it's a man. A really big man. With the light still shining in my eyes, it's almost impossible to make out the details of his appearance.

How am I going to identify my attacker in a lineup if I can't get a good look at him?

I'm two seconds away from locking myself in the bug when a gruff voice barks, "Poppy?"

MASON

*W*hen she remains frozen in place, staring at me like I'm an ax murder come to chop her up into tiny pieces, my temper explodes. "What the hell are you doing out here alone on the side of the road?"

She blinks as I eat up the asphalt between us with a handful of quick strides. I see the exact moment recognition dawns.

"Mason?" she whispers, relief flooding her voice as air rushes from her lungs.

"Yeah. You didn't answer the question. What are you doing out here at this time of night?"

She swallows, the delicate muscles of her throat constricting, before glancing at the Volkswagen. "I don't know what happened. It just died."

I shift my stance and look at the car. "Did any warning lights come on? Were there any noises right before it happened?"

"Um…" Her brow furrows as her teeth rake across her plump lower lip. "I don't think so."

I narrow my eyes. "Weren't you paying attention?"

Her gaze turns frosty as she straightens like I just rammed a two-by-four up her ass. "Of course I was paying attention, but I don't remember if there were any lights. One minute everything was fine, and the next, it's dead and I'm steering it to the side of the road."

"Are the keys still in the car?"

"No, they're in my purse. I was going to walk to my parents' house."

I can only stare as my temper explodes. "You were going to *what*?"

She raises a hand and points in the direction she'd just come from. "It's only a couple of miles away."

Every bad thing that could possibly happen to a woman walking alone on a dark, deserted road rolls through my head. It takes effort to keep my anger from breaking loose. "Is there a reason you wouldn't call your father to pick you up?"

Guilt flickers in her eyes before she glances away, mumbling something under her breath I can't quite decipher.

I cock my head and take a step closer. "What?"

She clears her throat and raises her voice. "I said that my phone is dead."

I drag a hand over my face. It's becoming more of a challenge to keep it together. "Are you shitting me right now?" Fury vibrates inside me like a live wire.

Even in the darkness with only the silvery moonlight and head-lights, I see the stain that suffuses her cheeks.

"Unfortunately, I'm not," she whispers.

"Do you have any idea how fucking dangerous this situation could have turned out?" Even though I'm doing everything in my power to keep my voice level, it escalates as I wave a hand. "You're wearing a tiny dress that barely covers your ass and your phone is dead, just like your car. What if I hadn't found you? What if some other guy with far fewer scruples had stopped and offered his help? What would you have done then?" My gaze skims over her curvy little body. "Fought him off? What do you weigh? A buck thirty?"

She smashes her lips together and scowls. "I'm twenty years old and already have a father. I'll get an earful from him when he finds out about this. I don't need to hear it from you, too."

My brows lower as smoke billows from my ears. "Well, that's too damn bad, little girl. You're gonna hear everything I have to say on the subject."

"I'm not a little girl," she says through gritted teeth.

"The fuck you aren't." And this just proves it.

Instead of responding, she crosses her arms tightly against her chest. It only makes her breasts swell against the tight fabric. The wave of desire that crashes over me has my dick rising with a vengeance.

I hold out my hand. "Give me the keys and I'll take a look. If it's not an easy fix, I'll call for a tow."

She reaches inside the car and grabs the keyring before setting it in my outstretched palm. A burst of unwanted energy jolts through my fingers as she does. Instead of meeting her gaze, which will only exacerbate the situation, I swing away before grabbing the handle of the door and yanking it open. I stare at the small opening in disgust before climbing inside. By the time I settle on the leather seat, it feels like my knees are shoved somewhere in the vicinity of my chin and I can barely move around in the tight space. Already I know it'll take a magic trick to get myself out of here.

I don't bother glancing at Poppy. If I do, I'll probably find a smile simmering around her lips. I can already feel the warmth of it radiating from her like sunlight.

"Don't say a word," I mutter.

She clears her throat. "I don't know what you're talking about."

Yeah, right.

I shove the key in the ignition and turn it, praying the engine starts up without issue.

Instead, I get nothing.

The damn thing won't even turn over.

Hmmm. If I had to guess, I'd say it's the starter or possibly a faulty alternator. I'm not even going to bother jumping it.

"Well?" She steps closer. "What do you think?"

Just like I suspected, it takes effort to unfold myself from this clown contraption she calls a vehicle.

Once free, I say with a huff, "I think it could be a couple of things. I'm going to tow it to my place and take a look over the weekend. It's probably the starter or alternator. There's an outside chance it could be the fuel pump. I'll have a better idea after I get under the hood." Before she can ask any more questions, I slide the cell from my pocket and call Jonny. He owns the towing service I use on a regular basis. I send business his way and he returns the favor.

My gaze reluctantly strays to Poppy as I give him all the details before hanging up.

"I didn't realize you were a mechanic."

Why that comment rubs me the wrong way, I have no idea. It takes all of five seconds to close the distance between us and push into her personal space. My voice cracks like a whip. "Do you have a problem with that?"

Her eyes flare. "Of course not. Why would you even ask?"

I jerk my shoulders.

Honestly, I don't know.

There's all this pent-up attraction buzzing around beneath the surface of my skin and nowhere for it to go. Instead of acknowledging that this girl has got me all hot and bothered, it's easier to snap and growl at her in hopes she'll keep a safe distance. It doesn't escape me that I'm the one who continues to move closer. I'm all but itching to get my hands on her. And that realization pisses me off more than anything else.

"Let me guess, you think a mechanic is beneath you."

Instead of cowering in the face of my anger, her eyes narrow as she squares her shoulders. "I never said that. You're being ridiculous."

When she takes a few cautious steps in retreat, attempting to put space between us, I stalk her on the deserted road. I can't stop myself. I just want to get my hands on her.

I raise a brow. "Am I?"

She bumps into the car and her spine flattens against the exterior. There's nowhere else for her to go. Nowhere left to run. Why that thought gets my blood pumping, I have no idea.

Or maybe I do.

It's just not something I want to inspect too closely.

"Yes." There's a beat of silence before she lifts her chin. "Are you this much of an ass to everyone or is it just me?"

Even though we're close, it's not enough to subdue the need rampaging dangerously inside me. I can't stop myself from pressing against her breasts until the warmth of her breath can ghost across my lips. I fucking hate how intoxicating it is. How it clouds my mind and better judgment.

All I want to do is inhale a giant gulp of her and hold it hostage in my lungs.

When I remain silent, she whispers, "Well?"

"It's just you."

Hurt and confusion flare in her eyes. "Why would you say that? What have I done?"

I'll tell you what she's done—the girl has invaded my every waking moment with thoughts of her.

Thoughts I shouldn't be having.

But how can I admit that?

"It doesn't matter," I growl. "Just stay the hell away from me. Got it?"

It seems almost impossible that her eyes could grow any larger, but that's exactly what happens. The truth seems to shock her into silence. Maybe now she'll finally leave me alone and everything in my life can once again return to normal. Exactly the way I like it.

When her tongue darts out to moisten pink-stained lips, my gaze reluctantly drops to the movement and a groan rumbles up from deep within my chest. That's all it takes for instinct to kick in and my mouth to collide with hers.

Even though I know I should stop, it's the furthest thing from my mind.

Unable to help myself, my tongue sweeps across the tight seam of her lips. When she doesn't immediately open, I nip at the lower one. A gasp escapes from her and I steal inside so that our tongues can tangle.

If I thought getting a taste of her would extinguish the harsh need careening through me, it does the exact opposite. If anything, it only stokes the flames burning brightly within. The very same ones I've been doing my damnedest to extinguish.

Her palms settle on my chest and I'm half-afraid she'll shove me away. Instead, her fingers curl into the cottony material of my T-shirt before tugging me closer. Her sweetness explodes on my tongue as I press myself against her soft curves.

The whimper that breaks free from her sends even more need roaring through my veins. My palm settles on her hip as the fingers bite into her flesh beneath before drifting upward, strumming over her belly. I continue to inch higher, sliding along her ribcage until I can graze the outer edge of her breast.

Fuck, but I bet she's soft all over.

I can't even begin to fathom what it would feel like to sink inside the warmth of her body.

As tempted as I am to lay my palm over her breast and squeeze, I resist the urge. Instead, my fingers ghost over her collarbone until they reach the base of her throat. There's a hitch in her breathing as my hand stills over the pulse that flutters madly like the wings of a hummingbird. My thumb and forefinger stroke over the delicate column until they're able to tighten around the curve of her jaw, while my other hand wraps around her hip to keep her firmly in place as our mouths stay fused.

In the blink of an eye, every bit of hard-fought self-control has fled. It wouldn't take much to slip my hand under the flirty little dress and yank her panties to the side so I can fuck her against the side of the car.

It's only the bright light of an oncoming truck that has my head clearing and my hands falling away from her delectable body. Even though I don't want to, I take a swift step in retreat, putting some much-needed distance between us. Poppy stares at me with eyes full of disbelief as one hand rises, grazing her swollen lips with the tips of her fingers, almost as if she can't believe that just happened.

Well...that makes two of us.

The tow truck rolls past before pulling in front of the bug and backing up.

"Go wait in my truck," I grunt, pissed at myself for allowing this to spiral so far out of control. "I'll deal with this."

When the driver's side door opens and Jonny jumps down, my gaze swings back to her. She's still flattened against the side of her car as if she needs it to keep her upright.

"Now," I growl, trying to prod her into movement.

She snaps to attention before her teeth scrape against her lower lip. It's like a shot straight to my dick, and it takes every ounce of self-control not to lay my hands on her for a second time.

"Hey, Mase," Jonny calls out in the darkness.

"Go on, Poppy. I'll be there as soon as this is taken care of."

She straightens and for a moment, I wonder if she'll argue. That's the last thing I need right now. Just as I step in her direction, she scrambles away, taking off for my truck. I huff out a breath before swiveling toward Jonny, only to find him staring at Poppy.

"Thanks for getting here so fast," I say, pulling his attention back to me.

He ignores the comment as a smile quirks his lips. "Pretty lady you've got there."

It's on the tip of my tongue to tell him that she's not mine, but I can already see interest brewing in his eyes. And I'll be damned if I stoke that fire.

"Thanks."

When I say nothing more, he turns to the VW and scratches his chin before giving me a bit of side eye. "Can't believe you'd date someone who drives one of these things."

My teeth are so tightly clenched that it's possible they'll shatter. "Do me a favor and tow it to my place."

"I'm curious…does she let you drive it?" There's a pause as he grins. "Cause I'd pay good money to see that."

Such a funny fucker.

Instead of responding, I toss him the keys. "Pull it right into the garage."

"You got it, man."

With that, I stalk to the pickup. My gaze locks on Poppy's as she sits in the passenger seat. I hate how much I like her there. What I need to do is drop her ass off and get the hell away from this girl before I do anything else I'll regret.

POPPY

$\mathcal{I}$ stare straight ahead as the truck barrels toward town. For the umpteenth time, my fingers rise to my lips before drifting over them in shock.

Has anyone ever kissed me quite so thoroughly?

It doesn't take much of a mental deep dive to come up with an answer. Most of the kisses I've received have either been tentative or lacking in any real passion.

This was the complete opposite.

It only took one brush of his lips to feel the pent-up aggression attempting to claw its way free. Almost as if it was a living, breathing entity. Honestly, the same kinds of feelings had coursed through me. Especially when he'd placed his hand at the base of my throat. His hold never tightened, the pressure never increased, but it was there just the same.

A constant reminder of his dominating presence.

I can't believe I'm even thinking this, but I liked it. I liked the way it made my heart thunder against my ribcage and my pulse quicken. There'd been something so commanding about his touch and the way he'd held my jaw captive in his grip.

I'd been so consumed by him that I hadn't realized the tow truck had arrived until he stepped away and cut off contact. I'd almost cried out, wanting to yank him back to me. It makes me wonder what sex with him would be like.

Rough?

Masterful?

Explosive?

Certainly nothing like the mediocre experiences I've encountered thus far.

I have the feeling that sex with Mason would be just as cataclysmic as our kiss. That thought sends a shiver dancing down my spine.

I sneak another peek at him from beneath the thick fringe of my lashes as he stares at the road stretched out beyond the windshield. His granite-like jaw is tightly clenched, and his fingers are wrapped around the steering wheel in a death grip. Other than ordering me into the vehicle when the tow service arrived, he hasn't spoken a word.

It's like I'm not even here.

I dredge my mind for something to say, something that will open up a line of communication between us, but it remains frustratingly blank. Mason isn't like any other guy I've met before, and I have no idea how to talk to him.

"What are you doing with Levi? Are you two going out?"

The barked-out question is like a gunshot in the silence of his pickup.

Go out with Levi?

It takes a couple of seconds for the words to penetrate the thick fog that clouds my brain.

Just as he flicks his steely gaze to me, I shake my head. "No."

"Is he aware of that?"

"Of course. We're friends."

"Is that what you really think?" There's a pause. "That you two are friends?"

"Yes, I do. We've known each other since freshman year."

"That doesn't matter," he says dismissively. "The guy wants way more than your friendship."

I swivel toward him. The thick haze that had fallen over me begins to dissipate, leaving me clearheaded. "How would you know?"

His jaw locks again. "Because I do."

One of my brows inches upward in annoyance as I wait for further explanation. When he remains stubbornly silent, I mutter, "I'm not sure why you care. It's none of your business."

From the corner of my eye, I see the muscle in his jaw tic to life.

"You need to stay away from the football players," he bites out before adding, "your father wouldn't like it."

Is this guy seriously trying to tell me who I can and can't be friends with?

Exactly who does he think he is?

"Actually," I snap, temper spiking, "my father *allows* me to make my own decisions."

"Well, I don't like it." He swings into the parking lot of my building and slides into a space near the front before shifting into park. He twists on the seat until his full attention falls on me.

It was so much easier to have this conversation when he was focused on the road. Now that his dark gaze is pinning mine in place, I feel like a deer caught in the bright glare of headlights. I'm frozen, barely able to suck in a breath.

"I don't care what you like," I force myself to whisper. "You don't make decisions for me."

A growl vibrates in his chest, making him sound more like a wild animal than the polite man who showed up to dinner a couple hours ago. Before I realize what's happening, his hand snakes out, wrapping around the nape of my neck. It doesn't take much effort on his part to drag me forward. As soon as he's within striking distance, his mouth crashes onto mine. Even though I'm surprised by the movement, I open. That's all it takes for his tongue to slip inside and tangle with my own.

For the second time this evening, fireworks explode inside my head.

Never in my life have I generated this kind of combustible energy with anyone. Until this evening, I had no idea it existed outside romance novels and movies.

That's the only thought ricocheting around in my brain as he assaults my senses, battering them like a raging storm. Kissing Mason is like having a war waged against you. He overwhelms me until it feels like I'm in danger of drowning in an ocean of desire.

Just when I question whether I can withstand another second of the onslaught, he pulls away enough to nip my lower lip with sharp teeth before sucking the plump flesh into his mouth. A whimper escapes from me as he delves back in for more. His tongue licks furiously at the inside of my mouth as if he's trying to taste every part of me.

Or maybe devour me one bite at a time until there's nothing left.

With a snarl, he releases me, pushing away until there's distance between us. His chest heaves as his breath escapes in short pants. It's as if we've both run a marathon.

I'm just as surprised by this kiss as I was the first time it happened on the deserted stretch of county road. My heart jackhammers an erratic tempo against my chest like a bird beating its wings against a cage.

I have no idea what to say in the heavy silence that unfolds.

"I'll take a look at your car after practice and let you know when it's fixed."

What?

That's it?

My mind cartwheels, trying to come up with a way to prolong this moment. More than anything, I want to understand why he kissed me. Especially when he told me not more than twenty minutes ago that he wanted me to stay away from him.

"Do you need my number?"

When his gaze darts to mine, I feel the intensity of it straight down to my toes. It only lasts a second or two before he breaks eye contact. "I'll let Coach know what happened and he can pick it up."

An irrational amount of disappointment floods through me.

When I continue to stare, half-tempted to argue that he doesn't need to involve my father, he says, "You should go. It's late."

My fingers tremble as they grip the handle before jerking on it. The door creaks open, and I have to force myself to exit the vehicle. My legs are strangely wobbly as they find the pavement. It takes a couple of seconds to steady myself before slamming the door shut and placing one foot in front of the other until I reach the entrance of the lobby. Even though I haven't looked over my shoulder, I know Mason is there, watching every move. I feel the heat of his gaze licking over me as I slip inside the apartment building.

It's only when the glass door slams behind me that I lose my internal battle and glance at the truck still idling in the lot. From across the distance that separates us, our gazes fasten and, for a heartbeat, I feel the connection we always seem to generate. I'm knocked from the trance when his truck roars to life and he backs out of the parking space, speeding off into the night.

If I were smart, I'd do just as Mason instructed and stay far away.

But that's the problem.

I'm not smart.

Because all I can think about is the next time I'll be able to feel his lips on mine.

MASON

hat the hell had I been thinking when I decided to tow her car to my place?

Oh, that's right.

I hadn't been.

It's not even noon and already I can tell the day will be a scorcher. I drag my forearm across my brow to wipe away the sweat that's sprung up before grabbing a socket wrench and loosening the spark plugs on the Ford Escape I'm working on.

I should have towed her car to Leon's, the garage I used to work at before I branched off on my own. Now that I'm coaching and going to school, I don't have as much time to get my hands dirty. If I take on more than I can chew, I send the overflow to him. We parted on good terms, and he appreciates the extra business.

When more sweat beads my brow, I grab the hem of the T-shirt and pull it over my head before wiping my face with it and then shoving part of the fabric into my back pocket. Even with three fans oscillating in the pole barn, I'm sweating my ass off. Thank fuck I rolled out of bed early this morning and came out here to work. In an hour or so, the sweltering temperature will be unbearable.

Once the spark plugs are changed, I tighten them and slam the hood shut. I need to get started on a Chevy Trailblazer and then hit the books. I'm still trying to find my groove with homework and studying. Once you've been out of school for a while, it's not easy to get back into that mindset again.

I wipe my palms against my jeans and beeline for the fridge to grab a beer. It might be a little early, but I don't give a shit. I need some liquid refreshment to take the edge off. Popping the top, I take a long swig.

There's nothing better than a cold brew on a hot day.

Well…maybe that's not altogether true.

I can think of something else that would be better. Maybe if I'd stuck to the plan the other night when I'd decided to hit the bar, I wouldn't feel so tightly strung today. There'd been a few women who'd strayed from their pack and attempted to strike up a conversation. One in particular had ticked all my boxes—pretty, curvy, and interested. It shouldn't have taken more than a drink or two before suggesting we head back to her place.

Instead, I'd dragged my heels before telling her I was tired and needed to take off. By her confused expression, she'd been just as surprised by my blurted-out comment as I was. I'd stalked out of the bar, aggravated with myself before sliding behind the wheel of the truck and gunning it out of the gravel parking lot. Not even ten minutes later, I'd found the very girl who had turned my night to shit stranded along the side of the road.

With a dead cell phone.

Wearing a little sundress that hugged her body.

And flimsy sandals.

Prepared to walk three miles back to her parents' place in the dark.

Can you even fucking imagine?

What the hell would have happened if I hadn't come along?

It had taken every ounce of self-control not to turn her over my knee before blistering her ass for being unprepared. Where was her phone charger, flares, or extra clothing?

How about a fucking flashlight?

Or even some kind of weapon or can of pepper spray?

The thought of something happening to her makes me gut sick. Had I left with that woman from the bar, I wouldn't have stumbled across her or been able to make sure she arrived home safe and sound.

What I shouldn't have done is kiss her.

Twice.

That had been a mistake.

Pressing myself against her body had been an even bigger one. And running my hand over her curves before wrapping it lightly around her throat and jaw had been the biggest one of all.

I tighten the same hand into a fist, still able to feel the flutter of her pulse beneath my fingertips. It had turned my dick to stone. Thank fuck Jonny arrived when he did, or who knows how far the situation would have spun out of control.

I'm knocked from those thoughts when a car rolls up the gravel drive. It must be Coach. I mentioned what happened at practice yesterday morning. He'd clapped me on the shoulder and thanked me profusely.

Honestly, after everything the man has done—not only for me but Hunter as well—it's the least I could do. I texted him about an hour ago to let him know that her Beetle was all set. Just like I'd suspected, a faulty alternator had been the culprit. It was a quick repair and there shouldn't be any more problems.

When the car door slams shut, I set the beer on the counter, expecting Derek to waltz into the garage. Instead, I find Poppy wearing tiny white shorts and a tank top that hugs her curves. My hungry gaze slides down the length of her before I can stop myself. On the way back up, it settles on her breasts. As I continue to stare, her nipples tighten into hard little points that poke through the thin material, and my dick twitches in response.

I force my attention away. "What the hell are you doing here?"

She arches a brow. "Dad said the car was ready to be picked up."

"I figured he'd come himself."

From the corner of my eye, I watch as she shakes her head and wanders further inside the barn that has been converted into a garage complete with lifts and a shit ton of tools.

"Nope. He was busy." When she glances at me again, our gazes locking, I feel the electrical current straight down to my toes. "Is that a problem?"

I grit my teeth.

Fuck yeah, it's a problem. I don't want this girl anywhere near me. Without even realizing it, she pushes all my buttons.

Buttons I had no idea existed.

"Let me get your keys and you can take off." The faster I hustle her ass out of here, the better off we'll both be.

"All right," she says with a careless shrug, taking in the car I've been working on. "Seems like you're busy."

"I am." I release a breath, relieved we're on the same page. Five minutes tops and she'll be long gone.

I nab her keys from the bench before swinging around again. As I do, her gaze falls to my bare chest and I still, unconsciously allowing her to look her fill. Every muscle tightens as air gets trapped in my lungs, making it impossible to breathe. A suffocating silence falls over us as the energy in the barn ratchets up, turning oppressive.

What is it about this girl that drives me so crazy?

One look at her in the locker room and I knew deep in my bones that she would be trouble.

Unfortunately, I wasn't wrong.

I wish to hell I had been.

In the short amount of time I've known Poppy, she's become impossible to evict from my brain. And touching her the other night, kissing her sweet lips, has only made it more of a struggle.

"Hey Pop, you want me to wait around and make sure you get back to your apartment?"

The moment is shattered as my gaze cuts to Levi, who loiters in the wide doorway. His gaze settles on the blonde before bouncing to mine.

"Hey, Coach." He lifts his hand in a wave before glancing around. "Cool shop."

What the fuck is he doing here?

"Thanks," I grumble, glaring at the QB.

"You know, I took a few auto mech classes in high school." He puffs out his chest and focuses his attention on Poppy. "I can change your oil anytime."

"Good to know," she says with a smile.

"It's already been done," I bite out, hating the idea of him doing anything for her. Can't she see it's just a ploy to get closer? "Any fluids that needed to be changed were taken care of and the rest were topped off."

"Well…I can do it next time." He gives her a wink along with a grin. "I won't even charge you."

She nods but remains silent. Her gaze flickers from him to me.

This little punk needs to get the hell out of here before I totally lose my shit. What the hell is he doing, sniffing around Coach's daughter? Poppy might think their friendship is purely platonic, but he doesn't. The hunger lurking in his eyes when he stares at her is clear as day.

I probably recognize it because I feel it, too.

Unlike him, I don't want to.

"You can take off, Levi. I took her car out for a test drive earlier and it's all good. There won't be any problems."

Ignoring the suggestion, he glances at Poppy for confirmation. Her gaze stays fastened to mine.

A tense silence follows before she says, "It's fine. You can take off." When she rips her gaze away, the sense of loss that hits me is like a punch to the gut. "Thanks for the ride, I appreciate it."

"It wasn't a problem." He shifts his stance before inching closer. "If you're not busy, I was thinking we could hang out for a while."

My muscles stiffen, and it takes every ounce of self-restraint not to bellow at him to get the hell out of my garage before I do bodily harm. It wouldn't take much prodding.

"I wish I could, but I'm slammed with homework."

He perks up. "We could study together."

"It probably won't work out this time, but maybe a different day?"

"Sure. It's a date."

The guy looks crestfallen at getting shut down.

His gaze darts to me before sliding back to her. "Okay then, I guess I should get moving."

She nods. "I'll see you in class tomorrow."

"Sounds good." He glances at me. "Bye, Coach."

I jerk my chin. "Catch you at practice."

When he reaches the door, he glances over his shoulder, giving Poppy one last look of longing before disappearing outside into the bright sunshine. Another silence descends, heightening the tension that hangs in the air.

It's only when the engine roars to life and the tires crunch over the gravel as Levi drives away that I snap, "Didn't I tell you the other night to stay the hell away from that kid?"

POPPY

My panties dampen at the way he growls out those words. His anger and prickly attitude shouldn't be a turn-on, but they are. Oh god, are they. The way his teeth clench, flashing in the light, and the muscle in his jaw tics against his sun-kissed flesh does strange things to my insides. His eyes ignite with a mixture of fury and something else I can't quite identify.

Lust?

Desire?

Exactly how far would I need to push for him to lose control again?

If that happened, would he kiss me like the other night?

A thick shiver of desire slides through me just remembering the way his lips took possession of mine. It was passionate, controlling, and nothing short of addictive. More than anything, I want to feel it again.

He takes a swift step forward, swallowing up a bit of distance between us before slamming to a halt. It's almost as if he's hit an invisible wall that stops him from moving closer.

"And I'm pretty sure I told you that I can do what I want."

His eyes narrow. "You brought him here to deliberately rile me up, didn't you?"

It's only when he fires off the question that I realize he's right. That's exactly what I did.

Lifting my chin, I straighten to my full height. "Yes."

Surprise morphs across his features.

Good. Maybe it's possible to knock him off balance the same way he does to me.

"Why?"

I jerk my shoulders. "Because I knew it would piss you off."

"And for some reason that seemed like a good idea?"

Before I can even open my mouth, he's on the move again. By the time he grinds to a halt, he's so close I can feel the warmth of his breath ghosting over my lips. The magnetic pull I feel for him has my body swaying forward. Instead of giving into the urge, I hold still, maintaining distance even though it's the last thing I want.

It's so tempting to lie but I've never been one to hide my true feelings or play games. Although, I've never blurted them out to a man who's practically a stranger. This is new terrain for me and it's nothing short of terrifying. The only other option is to keep them contained, and I can't do it any longer.

I straighten my shoulders and force out the truth. "Maybe because I wanted you to kiss me again, and this seemed like the easiest way to accomplish it."

A long, guttural groan escapes from him as his nostrils flare. If I didn't know better, I'd think the man was in agony.

The other night, he took my mouth like a conquering hero. Today, his lips hover over mine, barely touching them. I tilt my chin upward, attempting to get closer. For a long, drawn-out moment, we hang in suspension. He doesn't back away, but he doesn't take it any further.

The anticipation all but kills me.

Just when I think he'll dive in and take my mouth, he rips himself away until there's at least ten feet to separate us. I feel the distance with every fiber of my being.

He plows a rough hand through his hair before glaring. "You know nothing can happen between us, right?"

The question has my heart constricting. "Why not?"

His scowl intensifies. "For one, your father is my boss."

"And two?"

"You're too damn young." His gaze slides slowly down the length of my body before he rips it away and swears a blue streak under his breath. "Do you realize that I'm seven years older than you? For fuck's sake, you're still in college."

"So are you," I point out with a smirk, hoping to lighten his darkening mood.

His lips flatten as if he doesn't find that comment the least bit amusing. "I'm taking a couple of classes while I work. That's not the same as being a full-time college student. We're in totally different places and…" There's a pause. "I'm too damn old for you."

"Who says?"

"I do," he snaps, voice growing hard.

"What if I don't agree?"

When he remains silent, I cautiously close the distance until we're once again standing toe to toe. I have to tilt my neck to hold his gaze. There is so much suppressed heat and anger churning in his dark depths. The hot sparks that fly from his eyes nearly singe me alive. He's like a wild animal that needs to be tamed with a gentle touch.

Even though I'm desperate to soothe the hurt that lurks within him, I keep my hands glued to my sides. The more time that ticks by, the harder it becomes. When I can't resist the temptation any longer, I cautiously reach out and place my palms against the bare skin of his chest. He's hot to the touch as the muscles tense beneath my fingertips. There's a part of me that's afraid he'll bolt.

When he remains still, I stroke my hands upward, over chiseled pectorals before allowing them to drift downward. My hungry gaze tracks every movement, committing the moment to memory.

His body is beautiful.

I wish I could take my time and explore all of him.

"Poppy," he grits out, breaking into my thoughts.

"What?" I glance up and meet his gaze. The intensity nearly scorches me alive.

"You need to stop." His voice is strung impossibly tight, as if it'll snap at any given moment.

"Why?"

"Because I don't want to lose control."

"What if that's exactly what I want?" I pause before admitting, "I can't stop thinking about what it would be like if you just let go."

That's all it takes for a growl to vibrate in his chest as one hand snakes around the nape of my neck. Barely is there time for a gasp to escape as I'm dragged forward and his lips crush mine.

MASON

I *can't stop thinking about what it would be like if you just let go.*

Those fifteen words arranged into a sentence are what finally snap my tightly harnessed control. Without thinking, I leap forward to take what I've spent the last thirty-six hours obsessing about.

Even as my mouth roves over hers, I know this is a terrible idea. And yet, that knowledge isn't enough to stop the moment from unfolding.

Instead of being a passive participant like the other night, she kisses me back with an equal amount of fervor. That only stokes the flames of my desire. My cock is so hard it feels like it'll explode any second. I can't remember the last time a woman turned me on to this degree.

Maybe never.

It's a disturbing thought. One that gets shoved away before it can take root inside my brain and do permanent damage.

When she nips at my lower lip, everything circling viciously through my head vanishes until this girl is all I'm cognizant of. My hands go to her ass to lift her body. Her legs tangle around my waist as her arms tighten their hold. From this angle, I have to crane my neck to meet her mouth.

I walk us to the long stretch of counter before holding her up with one hand and clearing the paperwork and tools with the other. Everything scatters to the floor. The metal that clinks against the cement barely penetrates the thick haze clouding my brain.

My fingers go to the hem of her tank, stripping it away in one swift movement. When she doesn't protest, I slip my hands around her back and unhook the latches of her bra until the silky cups fall away. Need spikes through me as I grab the undergarment and toss it to the floor.

My gaze drops to her breasts, licking over the rounded flesh. She's bigger than I suspected. Slightly more than a handful topped with perfect little nipples that have hardened into tight points and beg for my attention.

Unable to resist any longer, I lean forward and catch one pert tip with my lips. A whimper escapes from her as she reclines against the linoleum, propping herself up on her elbows and arching her back as if she's making an offering. Minutes pass before I release the puckered bud with a soft pop and move to the other before gently biting down on the firm flesh.

When a gasp breaks free, I lave the stiff peak with my tongue before drawing it inside my mouth and sucking greedily.

My dick is so painfully hard that it feels like I'm in danger of exploding. I'm desperate to believe it's because I haven't been with a woman in a couple months, but deep down, I suspect that's not the reason. I think it has everything to do with the beautiful girl falling apart in my arms.

When the need to touch more of her thrums through me, I release the tight bud before nipping and kissing my way down her ribcage, past the soft curve of her belly until I reach the waistband of her shorts.

I'm so fucking close to the juncture of her thighs that the scent of her arousal teases my nostrils. My mouth practically salivates for a taste. All I can think about is ripping off every piece of clothing, spreading her lips, and lapping at her softness until she has no other choice but to scream out an orgasm.

My fingers slip beneath the band, arcing across her skin from one hipbone to the other before drifting back again. After several passes, I hesitate over the silver button and glance up. I've never been one to seek out permission, but with Poppy it feels imperative. Maybe it's because she's so much younger. Or that she's Coach's daughter.

Fuck.

I shove that thought from my brain before it can do permanent damage.

When I remain motionless, she lifts her head and opens her eyes until our gazes can lock.

"Should I stop?" I rasp.

"Don't you dare."

The throaty response does the impossible and has my lips lifting into a slight smile.

That's all the encouragement I need to flick open the button before dragging down the zipper. The grind of metal teeth breaks the silence of the garage. Once the material loosens, I work it over the rounded curve of her hips. She braces on her elbows, lifting her ass off the counter until the material puddles around her ankles and she's able to kick it away.

And then she's left in nothing more than pale blue panties.

Instead of delving in and shredding the fabric the way every instinct is urging me to do, I give myself a moment to take in the pretty picture she makes, lounging practically naked on the counter of my garage as bright sunlight pours in from the open door. I don't think I've ever seen anything more gorgeous than Poppy. The lust filling her heavy-lidded eyes only fuels my own.

Unable to wait a second longer, I slip my fingers beneath the elastic band and lower it. Part of me wants to tear the panties away until she's completely bared to my sight. But I can't deny there's something delicious about drawing out this moment.

The anticipation.

The thrill.

The way my pulse picks up tempo as my fingers tremble from the need rushing through my veins. It's like unwrapping a highly anticipated present at the crack of dawn on Christmas morning.

The toy you just knew would be fucking amazing.

That's exactly what this feels like.

I lower the cottony material, revealing her pussy one gorgeous inch at a time. When the thin fabric is wrapped around her thighs, impatience bursts inside me and I yank it away with a growl, leaving her naked.

My fingers settle on each ankle before gliding upward, stroking over well-defined calves along with the delicate flesh hidden behind her knees. A handful of seconds later, I finally reach her inner thighs. The need to glimpse all of her pounds through me as I flatten my palms against her soft skin and press her legs apart until she's stretched wide.

Air leaks painfully from my lungs.

I don't think I've ever seen anything as stunning in my entire life. When I run the pad of my thumb from the top of her slit to the very bottom, she arches into my touch, seeking out more.

So.

Damn.

Responsive.

Barely have I touched her, and she's already slick with arousal.

A tortured sound escapes from me as I give her pussy a long lap, retracing the path of my thumb before circling her clit with my tongue. With a moan, she tilts her pelvis, silently begging for more.

Repeating the maneuver, I dip inside her heat.

"You taste so fucking sweet," I groan, wondering how I'll ever get enough to satisfy my cravings. It doesn't seem possible. All I want to do is bury my face against her pussy and not come up for days.

Weeks.

Months.

My hands are positioned against her inner thighs to hold them apart. The thumbs touch the outer edges of her lips, pulling the soft flesh wider, opening her up until I can see and lick every delicate pink inch.

Her breath hitches as her muscles tense, turning impossibly tight.

Trying to keep all of my baser instincts under strict lock and key shreds my willpower. I've always prided myself on my determination, but this girl is showing me that it's nothing more than a paper-thin façade. Instead of attacking her flesh, I keep every lick, every caress at a steady tempo, knowing it's what will have her splintering apart before exploding.

I'm not wrong.

It doesn't take more than thirty seconds before she's crying out, her pussy spasming with pleasure. Her inner muscles contract, shuddering around me as I spear my tongue deep inside her body. With my face buried against her heat, I lick the damp flesh until her orgasm dissipates and her muscles turn slack. Only then do I lift my head and meet her dazed expression.

My dick is harder than steel with the need to bury myself balls deep inside her body. One touch and I'll come undone. Straightening to my full height, I flick open the button of my jeans and lower the zipper.

A condom.

I don't have one.

Fuck!

Usually I carry one in my wallet but didn't bring it out to the barn.

I mean…why would I?

It's not like I planned for this to happen. I sure as shit don't keep rubbers in here on the off chance a gorgeous woman might saunter in and we end up fucking on the counter. In the past, if one did so happen to wander into my workspace, I've been quick to send them on their merry little way.

From the first moment I caught sight of Poppy, I knew she was different. There's something about her that attracts me like a magnet.

"Mason?"

Her soft voice cuts through the chaotic whirl of my thoughts.

My gaze jerks, fastening onto her. She's still spread open. Only now, she's soft and swollen from her orgasm.

More blood rushes to my cock, making it impossible to think straight.

Fuck.

Fuck.

Fuck.

"I don't have a condom," I ground out. It's so tempting to wrap my hand around my cock and squeeze the tip to relieve some of the pressure. Otherwise, I'm half afraid the damn thing might blow off. I can be one of those horrific stories you see on *Sex Sent Me to the ER*.

"There's one in my purse." She points to the little pink bag lying haphazardly on the floor ten feet from the counter.

Funny…I didn't even notice she dropped the thing when I hauled her against me. Three long-legged strides are all it takes to reach the bag. With a glance speared in her direction, I hold it out.

"It should be in the side pocket."

For a second, our gazes stay locked. If there's one thing I've never done before, it's rummage around in a woman's purse. When I remain still, unsure what to do, she arches a brow. I blow out a steady breath before cautiously opening the flap and peeking inside. It's like getting a glimpse behind the curtain.

Just like she claimed, there's a foil packet tucked in the side pocket. I pull it free with my fingers. Instead of dropping the bag to the concrete, I toss it beside her as I return to the counter.

Once I've ripped into the square package with my teeth, I take out the lubricated rubber. Trust me, it's not needed. I'm so jacked up that I don't even bother to shed my jeans or boxers. Instead, I grip the waistband of my underwear and jerk it down so my dick can spring free. In one swift movement, I sheath my erection in latex and glance at her again. Excitement rushes through my veins before crashing over me, threatening to suck me under.

Already I know this won't take long.

That *I* won't last long.

How could I when I've never been this turned on in my life?

Just to be clear, I've had my fair share of women over the years and not once have I ever felt this kind of burning need to fuck. It's like a red haze has fallen over me, making it impossible to think straight.

I glance at her face, only to find her blue gaze pinned to my erection. She whimpers as her legs widen in silent invitation. If I was looking for a signal to proceed, I have it.

One quick step forward brings me close enough to line up the head of my cock with her slick entrance. For a fleeting second, I savor the harsh need pumping through me, making me feel more alive than I have in a long time. It wouldn't take much for this to become addictive.

For *her* to become addictive.

It's strange to have all this riotous emotion rampaging through me when I've done my damnedest to dull everything inside. All the grief and heartache from my parents' deaths and then the disappointment of dropping out of college and being forced to give up the sport I loved in order to raise my younger brother. I ignored the crushing weight, refusing to dwell on the emotions that came along with it. The bitterness of giving up my own dreams to help Hunter attain his...and then the grief when he cut me out of his life with the precision of a scalpel.

There've been rare bits and pieces of goodness along the way, but I've never allowed myself to feel that either. It didn't take long to realize that you can't have one without the other. It's just easier to get through life when you're operating on autopilot, numb to the world around you.

I have no idea why all these emotions are trying to claw their way to the surface when I'm on the cusp of fucking this girl, but that's exactly what's happening. And there doesn't seem to be a way to force them down again.

For better or worse, they're out there, floating around in the atmosphere.

Even though I've only buried myself an inch or two inside her tight heat, it's more than enough for pleasure to suffuse every cell of my being. I don't think I've felt this alive in years. It's as frightening as it is invigorating. Part of me wants to shy away and retreat to the relative safety of the darkness, while the other wants to run toward it with open arms.

I'm unsure which instinct will win out.

All I know is that I need to fuck this girl into oblivion.

Hopefully, it'll be enough to get her out of my system.

Pushing the confusing tangle of thoughts from my head, I focus on the place where we're intimately connected and watch as I thrust my hips until my length disappears inside her body. Intensity crashes over me, battering my senses like waves against a rocky coastline. Each one hammers at me, chipping away at the walls I've erected over the years to protect myself. I'm not even all the way inside her and it feels like I'm on the verge of exploding.

She's so fucking tight.

Like a glove.

I don't understand what this girl is doing to me. All these thoughts and feelings whipping through my body...they're in no way normal. They're not who I am. I've always been able to keep an emotional distance when I'm with a woman.

Fucking has always been just that...*fucking*.

But with her, an unwanted shift is occurring.

Already, I feel her inner muscles clenching around me, trying to draw me farther inside her body. It's a struggle not to give in and pummel her pussy until I explode.

Inch by inch, I sink inside her until I'm finally buried to the hilt. Until I'm lightheaded and unable to think straight. With gritted teeth, I force myself to slide out again before driving forward. A moan escapes from her as my movements ramp up. My arms snake around her until each palm is filled with the rounded curves of her ass. I drag her forward until we're pressed together. Only then do I give myself over to my instincts and fuck her the way I've been dreaming about. My hips piston as she wraps her legs tightly around my waist so that she's splayed completely open.

The groan that escapes from me is deep and guttural.

As tempting as it is to squeeze my eyes tight and bask in the intensity of these newly awakened feelings, I don't.

Can't.

I need to see every flicker of emotion as it flashes across her face. I know what she does to me. I need to see what I do to her in return.

With every thrust, a little more of my self-control slips away. My jaw locks as I force myself to last longer than a dozen strokes.

But I can't.

It's not working.

It's only a matter of time before I—

When her pussy clenches around me and a cry tears from her lips, I lose total control. It's like an out-of-body experience. I'm pretty sure the tip of my cock explodes with the sheer force of my release as stars burst behind my eyelids. My orgasm seems to last forever. Wave after wave of pleasure crashes over me, threatening to drag me to the very bottom of the ocean. The force of it sucks every molecule of oxygen from my lungs.

We stay fused together, our labored breathing echoing throughout the quietness of the garage. It's only when I soften and her pussy stops spasming that a prick of regret nudges its way inside my brain. Her legs are still wrapped tightly around my waist, locking me to her, as I try to summon enough energy to move.

I search the far recesses of my brain, wondering if I've ever come that hard in my life.

The answer is terrifying.

The very last thing I want is for this girl to be any different from the ones who've come before her.

As soon as the thick haze infiltrating my brain dissipates, I pull out of her warmth and break eye contact, no longer able to meet her gaze. At a loss for words, I turn away, tucking myself back inside my boxers and hauling up my jeans before disposing of the condom in the trashcan a dozen feet away.

As soon as the lid slams shut on the garbage, the gravity of the situation slams into me, knocking the air from my lungs.

I plow a hand through my hair before swinging around to face her.

It feels like there's a lump of wet sawdust wedged in the middle of my throat as I force myself to meet her gaze. Maybe reality has hit me with the force of a sledgehammer, but it's not the same for Poppy. She still looks blissed out of her mind. I have to fight the urge to close the distance and gather her up into my arms.

Instead of giving into my instincts, I say, "You should probably get dressed."

POPPY

ou should probably get dressed.

Those five words are all it takes to snap me out of the thick sexual fog that has descended. They're like a sharp slap across my face as I blink back to awareness and realize I'm still sprawled naked on the counter in Mason's pole barn while he stares dispassionately at me. Heat floods my cheeks as I attempt to kick my brain into gear and scamper off the long stretch of linoleum.

As my bare feet hit the concrete, I avert my eyes and drop down to grab my panties before hauling them up my legs. Snapping up my bra, I chance a peek at Mason. He's turned away so that the wide expanse of his bare back faces me.

Is he so repentant that he can't even meet my eyes?

That's all it takes for fury to explode inside me.

I pick up the shorts and tank before covering myself. Once I've slipped my sandals on my feet, I glance around for my purse before nabbing it from the counter. It's only when I'm fully dressed that I clear my throat.

If Mason thinks I'm going to slink away in embarrassment so he doesn't have to acknowledge what happened, he couldn't be more

67

wrong. Even before he pulled out of my body, I caught a glimpse of the regret churning in his eyes.

The silence in the garage turns oppressive as he reluctantly turns and our gazes collide.

It's disheartening to realize that I wasn't wrong about the regret. It's there, overpowering everything else swimming around in his dark depths. The passionate man from moments ago is now long gone, almost as if he'd never been there to begin with, and the previous twenty minutes were nothing more than a figment of my overactive imagination.

I lift my chin higher and hold his gaze. I've never played the part of shrinking violet, and I refuse to do it now.

"That was a mistake," he mutters.

Ouch.

The one thing I've never been called is a mistake.

Although, in all honesty, it's not like I didn't see this coming from a mile away.

I tilt my head and force myself to remain calm. "You think so?"

Storm clouds gather in his eyes. "You know it was." He shoves a hand through his hair for a second time before breaking eye contact. "Look, I'm sor—"

"I don't want your regret," I say sharply, cutting him off.

Him trying to apologize for giving me the best orgasm of my life is just the icing on the cake.

He glances away as remorse flickers across his expression. It's obvious from his reaction that he has no idea what to say or how to smooth over this situation.

Unwilling to stand here for another second, I snap, "How much do I owe you for the repair?"

His surprised gaze darts to mine. If he was expecting me to throw a tantrum or cry and pout, it'll be a cold day in hell before that happens. I have way too much self-respect for that kind of behavior.

"Um, nothing. It was just your alternator. I had a spare one sitting around the shop. So, it's all good."

It's so tempting to argue.

I don't want to be beholden to this man for anything.

Instead, I jerk my head into a tight nod and hold out my hand.

When he stares at my palm in confusion, I say, "I'd like my keys."

"Um, yeah." Something I can't quite decipher flickers across his expression before he swings away, stalking to the counter. Hanging above the length of linoleum is a key holder with three sets dangling from it. He grabs the middle one before swallowing up the distance until he's close enough for his woodsy aftershave to tease my senses. It takes effort to steel myself against the intoxicating scent and not inhale a big breath into my lungs.

"Here you go," he says.

Without making contact, I grab the keys before whirling away and stalking toward the exit. Even though I was raised with manners, I can't bring myself to say thank you.

"Poppy," he rasps as I reach the door.

Hope rises reluctantly within me. Given his asshole behavior, I wasn't expecting him to stop me. My step falters as I glance over my shoulder and meet his gaze.

"Stay away from the kid."

And just like that, my heart crashes to the bottom of my toes.

Not bothering with a response, I stride out of the barn without a backwards look.

MASON

I manage to keep it together until her VW rolls down the gravel drive and turns onto the county road that leads to town. As soon as she's gone, I lose it. Bitter regret and anger churn in the pit of my gut before bubbling up like a geyser. I storm to the counter and grab her broken alternator before hurling it across the open space. It crashes against the barn wall before dropping to the concrete where it clanks, shattering the silence of the afternoon.

Fuck.

Fuck.

Fuck.

How stupid am I?

She wasn't even here for five damn minutes, and I couldn't hold it together without screwing her.

Here's an even better question—how the hell am I going to face her father after what just happened?

The anguish that escapes from my lips is cut off by a deep voice.

"That pissed off, huh?"

I swing around, only to find Hunter. My first impulse is to launch myself at his tall form and wrap my arms around him in a giant bearhug before squeezing the life out of him.

Instead, I stay rooted in place. It's tempting to rub my eyes and make sure this isn't some sort of strange hallucination. I haven't seen my brother since he left town with Skye after college graduation.

There've been a few stilted texts back and forth but nothing of consequence. Nothing to say that he's forgiven me and is ready to let me back into his life again. The closest I'm able to get is watching his games on TV and interviews on ESPN.

When I remain silent, he asks, "Does your mood have anything to do with the pretty blonde who just lit out of here like her ass was on fire?"

Yeah…that's not a question I'm going to touch with a ten-foot pole. Even if my brother and I were on the best of terms, I wouldn't want to discuss the messed-up situation with Poppy.

Refusing to tackle that issue, I turn the conversation back on him. "What are you doing here?"

With a shrug, he breaks eye contact before looking around the barn. "I heard Coach hired you as an assistant and that you're now taking a few classes at the university." He glances at me for confirmation.

"You heard right."

He nods and shifts his stance. "Not going to ask how I found out?"

My tongue slides across the front of my teeth. "I assume you talked to Coach."

"Yup. He seemed happy that you're working with his QB."

I rein in the snort before it can escape. I have the sneaking suspicion that damn kid is going to get his neck wrung before the end of this season. And it'll have absolutely nothing to do with football.

As I stare at my brother, I'm struck with the bizarreness of this conversation.

For so long, it was just the two of us pitted against the world. Plenty of friends and acquaintances offered a helping hand, but in the end, I refused to accept the assistance. We were able to get by on our own because we were together.

A team.

A unit.

And now look at us…engaging in a surface-level conversation like we're nothing more than strangers.

It sucks.

Instead of taking the bull by the horns and talking about what's really going on, I bury those thoughts and the pain they cause deep down inside where they can't see the light of day.

"I'm enjoying it."

"You still working on cars?" He moves farther inside the barn.

There used to be a time when Hunter would hoist himself onto the counter, and we'd shoot the shit for hours. After a long day spent in the garage, we'd crack open a couple of cold ones.

Back then, I didn't think anything could rip us apart. I thought our bond was tight. Solid. But it wasn't enough to withstand Skye. Ever since they got together freshman year of high school, she was all he could see.

All he could think about.

I'm not proud to admit it, but I let jealousy get the best of me.

Even though we both lost our parents, his life didn't come to a screeching halt the way mine did. He wasn't forced to drop out of college or stop playing the sport he loved. He didn't have to work full time to make ends meet and keep a roof over our heads. No matter how hard I busted my ass, we still lived on a shoestring budget. If Hunter needed new cleats, I went without or took on a few extra jobs at the garage to make sure he had them.

I worked weekends.

I put in ten- and twelve-hour days.

After our parents died, Hunter had Skye to cling to.

He had school and football.

Normalcy.

My life got turned upside down and inside out.

I should have handled it better.

What I've learned in the last two years since we've splintered apart is that regret is a cold-hearted bitch. Sometimes, there's nothing more you can do but make peace with your demons and move on. Otherwise, they'll eat you alive.

I sweep those depressing thoughts from my brain and focus on the conversation. "It pays the bills."

He nods before shoving his hands into the pockets of his jeans. "You know I'd give you money if you needed it. You've earned it, Mase. That was part of our agreement."

I jerk my shoulders and fold my arms across my bare chest. I'll be damned if I take one cent from him. "I'm doing just fine. You don't need to worry about me."

He searches my eyes with ones that are just as dark and penetrating. Staring at Hunter is like looking in the mirror.

"Still…"

When his voice trails off, an awkward silence descends that makes the cracks in our relationship even more apparent.

Uncomfortable with the lapse in conversation, I clear my throat. "Where's your better half?"

Emotion flickers across Hunter's face. "At her father's place, helping Brandi go through some of his stuff."

Well, shit. There's not much I can say to that. We had to do the same thing for our parents.

"I was sorry to hear about Dean," I mumble, shifting my weight from one foot to the other.

Hunter nods. "Thanks."

After the accident, Skye's father became more like a surrogate to him.

Until Skye left town.

"How's she handling it?"

He jerks his shoulders. "It's hard. They were close. Even though you know something is coming around the bend, and you think you're prepared for it, there's really no way to be ready for the void that person leaves behind in your life."

"No, I suppose there isn't." The pause that follows is filled with poignancy. My guess is that we're both dredging up the past and thinking about our own parents. We never had the chance to say goodbye to them. One moment they were here, heading out for a boat ride, and the next, they were gone. "Make sure you give her my best."

"I will. She'll appreciate it."

For just a few seconds, I'm almost able to fool myself into believing that everything's just like it used to be, but then another silence falls over us, reminding me that nothing is the same.

That it might not ever be the same.

"So…how's the team shaping up?" I ask.

The tension marring his expression dissolves. Shooting the shit about football has always been second nature for us. We could talk for days and still never run out of things to say.

"It's good. Hard." His voice dips. "Harder than I expected. It's the reason I called Coach. I needed to talk with him. Get his perspective on a few things."

As much as I wish Hunter's words didn't sting, they do. I'm the one he should be leaning on. Instead, I'm the last person he wants to discuss his problems with.

"Was he able to help?"

"Yeah, he did. I made some mistakes my rookie year. I just need to keep my head down and work hard."

My shoulders loosen. "Sounds like solid advice."

When neither of us keeps the conversational ball rolling, another thick blanket of tension falls over us.

He plows a hand through his short hair. "Look, Mase, I don't want it to be like this between us. It's been almost two years."

Hard to imagine, but it's true. Two fucking years without talking to my brother on the daily. And yet it seems so much longer.

There used to be a time when we were thick as thieves. Now, it feels like there's an ocean between us. He's on one side while I'm standing on the other.

I've apologized.

Dozens of times.

But it hasn't made a dent in his anger or resentment.

I'm not sure if anything will at this point.

Not even time.

The day he married Skye, I drank myself into a stupor right here in the garage. It was the second worst one of my life, after my parents dying.

"I don't either," I say softly, trying to hold my emotions in check.

With a nod, he glances away. Neither of us is very comfortable talking about our feelings.

I jerk my head toward the fridge. "You want a beer?"

He shrugs, looking grateful for the switch in topic. "Sure, I could have one."

I nod before swinging toward the fridge. Once there, I pull open the handle and grab two Miller Lites. Using the edge of the counter, I knock both caps off before handing one over to Hunter. He brings the long neck bottle to his lips and takes a swig. I do the same as he hoists himself onto the counter. For a second, what just happened there fifteen minutes ago flashes through my brain before I shake the memory away.

With the afternoon sunlight pouring in through the open door, we guzzle down half our bottles.

"So," he says, "I was thinking you could come out and watch one of my games this season."

My muscles still as everything inside me tentatively lifts. It takes effort to fight back the thick emotion gathering in my chest. "I'd like that." I shift, almost afraid to ask. "Are you sure Skye is good with it?"

It's weird to think that my baby brother is now a married man and has to run things by his wife.

"It was her idea," he says quietly.

My brows rise at the admittance.

That's not what I was expecting. Although, as much as I hate to admit it, Skye was always a nice girl. When I sent her packing, it was never personal.

With a jerk of his shoulders, he stares down at the bottle in his hand before picking at the white label with his thumbnail. "Yeah, the loss of Dean has hit her pretty hard." He glances at me. "Kind of puts things into perspective, you know?"

There's no way to swallow past the thick lump wedged in the middle of my throat. "Yeah, it does."

"Ever since Mom and Dad died, it's been the two of us. I thought it would always be that way." His voice drops as he unwittingly echoes my earlier sentiments. "You know they would hate that we've allowed this to happen."

I drag a hand over my face. Damn straight they would. And they'd lay the blame squarely at my feet, because that's where it belongs.

"I really am sorry for what I did, Hunt. If there were a way to go back and make different choices, I'd do it in a heartbeat."

His gaze falls to the brown bottle again. "I know. I just needed time to get over it."

"Have you?" I force out the rest of the question. "Have you gotten over it?" My heartrate kicks up its tempo, pounding uncomfortably in my chest.

He looks up, spearing me with dark eyes. "I think so."

Air escapes from my lungs in a rush. Only now do I realize that I've been holding it captive in my body. The backs of my eyelids burn, and I have to blink away the moisture that threatens to gather in my eyes. I'm unsure what to do with all these emotions that churn dangerously within me.

"Good." I shift my stance and force myself to say, "If you want me to talk with Skye—"

He shakes his head. "She wasn't the one with the problem. I was."

His words reach into my chest and rip my beating heart right out of my body.

"I know," I acknowledge softly. Skye was never the kind of girl to hold a grudge.

My brother, on the other hand?

Especially when it came to her?

I'm lucky it only took two years for him to come around.

"Are we good?"

His lips quirk at the corners. "I think we will be." He jerks his head toward the parking lot. "So...anything you want to tell me about the girl in the VW Beetle who just lit out of here?"

"Nope."

For the first time in years, he flashes a genuine smile. "Well hell, now I'm really curious."

POPPY

"Would you mind getting the door?" Anne asks, grabbing an oversized platter piled high with thick wedges of watermelon.

I pad to the slider that leads to the patio and yank it open. Dad is already outside, manning the grill. Even though it's early in the afternoon, there are already fifty people in attendance for the annual Claremont Cougars barbeque that will officially kick off the season.

Unconsciously, I scan the yard. The pool is packed with shirtless guys. Since they train all year round, most are in excellent shape. It's certainly no hardship to stare at them. I should be basking in man candy heaven.

Instead, my attention is continually snagged by the brooding man standing with a small group of coaches. He's barely glanced my way since arriving an hour ago.

It's been just about a week since the incident at his garage.

He slinks into Psychology before the start of class and hightails it out the moment our professor wraps up his lecture. After the disastrous way our encounter ended, it should be a relief that he's actively avoiding me, making it easier to pretend nothing happened.

It's not.

I'm sure part of it has to do with the fact that I've never orgasmed so hard in my life. So yeah…it's kind of difficult to stop reliving *that* particular memory like a slow-motion, Technicolor picture show.

Apparently, that's not the case for Mason.

I wasn't so much as a blip on his radar.

Then again, did I really expect anything different?

The man is twenty-seven years old and probably has a ton of experience where women are concerned. I'm twenty, and while I've had a few boyfriends, I'm not quite on the same level. It also sucks that when compared to Mason, all the guys I've slept with seem more like boys who didn't have a clue what they were doing. I've always suspected it, but being with someone who knows how to touch a woman to elicit the most pleasure has only slammed home that fact.

After getting a taste of what sex can be like when it's good, how am I supposed go back to college-aged guys who are more concerned with their own pleasure than mine?

It seems grossly unfair.

"Poppy?"

I blink back to the present and Anne, who stares from a few feet away with a furrowed brow. "Yeah?"

"Close the door before the bugs get in."

Heat scalds my cheeks as I nod, yanking the slider shut again.

Ugh.

I really need to snap out of this. Mason has moved on, and it would be in my best interest to do the same. If that thought fills me with disappointment, I shove it away, refusing to dwell on it.

All right…enough of this.

I suck in a deep, cleansing breath and paste a smile on my face before joining the party. First, I swing by the food table to make sure all the snack bowls have been replenished. Most of these guys are well over two hundred pounds—some over three—and they eat like they're heading into hibernation for the long winter months.

I make my way over to Dad and ask if he needs any help with the grill. He shakes his head in response. Yeah, I probably should have known better. Much like the football field, the grill is his domain, and he doesn't like people—by which I mean Anne or me—getting in his way.

"Hey, Poppy."

Levi saunters over with a couple of teammates.

"We were just about to get a game of water volleyball going. Any interest in playing?"

Just as he asks the question, the two guys he walked over with start pushing and shoving each other before taking off toward the pool and leaping into the water. A giant splash rises like a wave, dousing the people nearest to the edge.

"Maybe later. I've been recruited to make sure the bowls stay filled. Anne will have my head if I'm derelict in my duties." I say it like the job is a bother, but truthfully, I don't have any real interest in playing around with these guys. They're like puppies with too much pent-up energy.

"Yeah, sure. We can wait until later. No big deal."

I point to the pool where his friends are horsing around, attempting to drown one another. "It's hot out. You should join them."

He glances at the water and shakes his head. "Nah, I was kind of hoping we could spend a little time together. Whenever I hit you up to hang out, you're always busy."

I nip my lower lip between my teeth and glance away. He's not wrong about that. Every time Levi suggests grabbing something to eat or getting together to study, I come up with an excuse. Most of them are true. Now that the first few weeks of school are behind us, I'm buried beneath a mountain of homework, projects, and tests.

Could I make time if I wanted?

I suppose…the problem is that I don't necessarily want to.

I like Levi as a friend. He's funny and nice. After Mason made a big deal about the QB wanting more than friendship, I realized he was probably right. Since I don't want to lead him on, I've pulled back from spending time with him. I was hoping he'd get the hint so we wouldn't have to have a conversation about it.

When I remain silent, his voice drops so only I can hear. "Do you think we could go somewhere private and talk?"

"Umm…" I glance around the boisterous party, hoping to catch Dad or Anne's eyes so they can summon me over, but they're both busy chatting with guests. My shoulders slump with the realization that I won't be able to avoid this convo. "Okay."

"Great." He flashes a winsome smile before wrapping his fingers around mine and tugging me toward the pool house located near the back of the property.

Once we reach the small white structure, he pushes open the door and pulls me over the threshold before closing it behind us.

"This is way better. With the music and all the guys yelling, I could barely hear myself think." He points to the couch. "Want to sit?"

"Sure."

Levi drops onto the middle cushion. With no other choice, I settle gingerly next to him.

MASON

hat the actual fuck?

Did Poppy just disappear into the pool house with Levi?

I glance at her father only to see that he's deep in conversation with our defensive coordinator. He probably doesn't realize his daughter just went missing. Anne is busy checking out the food situation while she chats with one of the coaches' wives.

I drag a hand over my face and grit my teeth until my jaw aches from the pressure before glancing at my sports watch.

"Mason?"

"Yeah?" My attention reluctantly returns to Jason, another assistant coach. Honestly, I have no idea what the hell he's been yapping about. Maybe a new exercise regimen he wants to implement? I've spent the past hour covertly watching Poppy, all the while nodding and grunting at appropriate intervals.

I can't stop my gaze from dropping to my watch again. It's been three minutes since they shuttered themselves inside the structure.

What the hell are they doing in there?

Only one answer comes to mind.

My hands tighten at my sides.

"I asked what you thought about adding a nutritionist to make the guys protein shakes after practice as part of their active recovery."

I clap Jason on the shoulder. "I think you're definitely on to something."

"Really?" He perks up. "Should I mention it at the next meeting?"

"Nah. I'd talk to him about it right now."

His expression morphs into one of surprise as he shifts his stance and considers my advice. "You think so?"

"Absolutely." I point to Coach. "There's no time like the present."

"Thanks, Mason. I'll let you know how it goes."

"You be sure to do that."

As soon as Jason walks away, I take off for the pool house. It's been five minutes and counting. So help me god if I find the door locked. I'll bust the damn thing down. The thought of Poppy shuttered away inside with Levi sends my temper skyrocketing.

A few players attempt to catch my attention as I stalk around the rectangular-shaped pool.

"Hey, Coach! Want to—"

"Nope." I don't even bother making eye contact. I'm a man on a mission. And that mission is to disrupt whatever the hell is going on in that room. And maybe wring Levi's neck. That has yet to be determined.

The closer I get to the small building, the harder it becomes to contain my anger. Once there, I grab hold of the handle and yank with all my might. The door crashes against the wall before reverberating on its hinges. Levi startles, nearly jumping from the couch where he sits next to Poppy, before staring at me with wide eyes.

"Out!" I growl, jerking a thumb over my shoulder.

His brows slam together as his face scrunches. "Coach?"

"Get. Out." I grit those two words through clenched teeth. If the kid doesn't get his carcass moving, I'll gladly do it for him.

He shoots Poppy a questioning look as if she has any say in the matter.

"You should probably go," she murmurs. "We'll talk later."

Yeah...that won't be happening.

Levi flicks his gaze to me again, and I see the anger and confusion swimming around in his green depths. What's also clear is that he's desperate to argue.

When I take a menacing step toward him, he reluctantly rises to his feet before staring down at Poppy. That same look of longing that filled his expression at the garage returns. All it does is piss me off more than I already am.

"I'll catch you later," he mutters.

"Sounds good." She gives him a small smile.

With a glare, he jerks his head into a tight nod before stalking past me. Once he's crossed over the threshold, he stops, jerking around to stare at her again. Just as he opens his mouth, I slam the door in his face.

Poppy's eyes flare wide as one hand rises to her lips. "I can't believe you just did that," she whispers. "What's wrong with you?"

"Quite a bit." That—unfortunately—isn't a lie. I'm totally messed up in the head, and it has everything to do with the curvy blonde that refuses to be expelled from my brain. Before she can lay into me, I snap, "What the hell were you two doing alone in here?"

The shock clouding her expression fades as her lips twist into a scowl. "Nothing that concerns you." Anger floods her tone. "You might not believe this, but I'm a grown woman who can do what she wants."

I tilt my head and hold her glare as sparks of blue fire shoot from her eyes. I don't think I've ever seen her look more beautiful than she does at this moment, bristling with fury. All right, that's not true. The way she looked spread out naked on the counter in the garage is an image that will forever haunt me. No matter how many years pass by, it's not one I'll forget.

"Wanna bet?"

And then I'm on the move, stalking toward her. When I'm close enough, my hand shoots out, wrapping around her bicep and dragging her from the couch. As soon as she crashes into my chest, my arms snake around her body, locking her to me until I can feel every soft curve pressed against my harder lines.

What is it about this girl that drives me so fucking crazy?

I'm not used to my emotions simmering so close to the surface.

Or wanting someone like this.

"Actually, I would. You've been perfectly clear about not being interested."

"I never said I wasn't interested," I ground out reluctantly. "What I said is that you're too damn young for me and your father is my boss."

Her brows rise in challenge. "Neither one of those things has changed."

"Oh, trust me, I'm aware of that fact."

Her gaze stays pinned to mine. With the door closed, the music and voices from outside become muted. Her breathing picks up its tempo as the pulse beneath the delicate flesh of her throat flutters wildly.

"Is it just Levi you have a problem with or guys in general?"

The answer shoots out of my mouth before I can stop it. "Guys in general."

"That's going to be a problem. One you'll have to deal with."

"You're absolutely right," I agree. "I need to deal with the situation."

With that, my mouth crashes onto hers. Instead of opening under the firm pressure like I expect, her lips stay pressed together. A growl rumbles up from deep within my chest that she's even attempting to deny me her sweetness.

When I nip her lower lip with sharp teeth, she yelps. As soon as her mouth opens, my tongue delves inside to tangle with her own. Her hands slip between us before her palms flatten against my chest.

Instead of pushing me away, her fingers curl into the fabric of my T-shirt, attempting to drag me closer. Electricity sizzles in the air around us, and the party raging on the other side of the wall fades to the background. It's impossible to think about anything other than the feel of her in my arms.

As our tongues continue to stroke, my fingers drift to the hem of her shirt before clenching the fabric and dragging it over her head. Not once do the ramifications enter my brain as I flick open the button of her shorts and shove them down her hips and thighs.

When the material puddles around her ankles, she steps out of them.

I pull away just enough for my gaze to skim down the length of her body. Her breasts are practically overflowing from the tiny black bikini top. It's enough to bring a grown man to his knees.

"Were you really going to wear that in front of all those horny bastards?" Before she can respond, I rasp, "Are you seriously trying to kill me?"

Her lips twitch at the corners. "Yes to both questions."

A growl works its way up from deep within my chest. This girl has no idea what kind of animal she's unleashed within me. Even I'm unsettled by the depth of emotion that has been set free.

My hand snakes around her back before finding the strings that are tied against her spine. I yank the knot so the fabric loosens before hanging free. I swiftly do the same to the one at the nape of her neck until the bikini floats to the floor, leaving her bare breasted.

She's just as beautiful as I remember. I'm not going to lie, I'd hoped that maybe I'd built her up in my mind. Turns out that's not the case.

When she doesn't protest, my fingers settle on the twin ties at her hips. Two seconds later, the tiny scrap of material lands on top of the shorts.

A hiss of breath escapes from me as my hands rise to cup the heavy weight before plucking at the peaked nipples in tandem. That's all it takes for her eyelids to turn heavy and feather shut. As I advance, she takes a step in retreat until the backs of her knees hit the couch and she tumbles onto the cushion. Her gaze never strays from mine as I rip off my shirt before shoving down the shorts and boxers until I'm just as naked as she is. Already, my cock feels like steel. When her gaze drops to the thick length, it grows even harder.

"Are you sure about this?" I ask, voice tightly strung.

With a nod, her tongue darts out to moisten her lips. "I'm not the one who was unsure. You were."

She's right about that.

I reach down and grab my khaki shorts before searching the back pocket for my wallet and then a condom. I tear it open with my teeth and sheath myself in latex. Her gaze stays focused on me the entire time.

No matter what, I always want her eyes trained on me. I'm not even with this girl and it feels like I'm in so deep, I'll never fight my way free.

Unwilling to dwell on those disconcerting thoughts when I have her naked in front of me, I take her lips in a rough kiss. How is it that the only time I feel like I can breathe is when my mouth is fastened to hers?

It doesn't make a damn bit of sense.

Nothing about this situation makes sense.

But still…it doesn't change the way I feel. And it certainly doesn't stop all these strange emotions from multiplying every time we're together.

Even though there's a distant voice in the back of my brain telling me this is a shit idea, I force it away, refusing to listen. It only takes one swift stroke and I'm buried deep inside the heat of her body.

Fuuuuck.

Have I ever felt anything so damn good?

The only thought pounding through my head is that I'll never get enough of this.

Of her.

When a whimper slides from her lips, filling the sultry air, it stokes my need to a fever pitch. My balls tighten, drawing up against my body, and I grit my teeth, trying to hold it together. The last thing I want to do is blow my load before she comes.

Christ.

It's like I'm a horny teenager all over again.

The second her pussy contracts around me, my own orgasm breaks loose. Her soft cries mix with my grunts as stars explode behind my eyelids.

Fuck.

Fuck.

Fuck.

It's only when the last spurt of cum leaves my body that I press my forehead against hers. Our harsh breaths mingle, becoming one. I don't think I've ever exploded so fast in my life.

Barely did I get inside her before losing it.

As the silence of the pool house settles around us, the thick haze of anger and arousal clouding my mind clears enough for me to think straight.

It takes effort to summon my voice. "You realize your father is gonna kill me, right?"

She huffs out a laugh. "No, he won't."

"The hell he will. You're too damn young for me." There's a pause before I force out the truth. "You're practically a baby."

"Hardly. I'm a grown woman."

"Who is seven years younger," I say with a grunt.

She pulls away enough to search my eyes. "How about we take this one step at a time." There's a pause. "Maybe we can have dinner and see what happens."

I allow her words to roll around like marbles in my head before reluctantly giving in. "All right."

If I'm lucky, our date will turn out to be a total disaster and we'll have nothing in common. Just because we have chemistry in the sack doesn't mean a damn thing. It's entirely possible I jacked myself up for nothing.

Relief floods through me as I latch onto those thoughts with the desperation of a drowning man. Just as my muscles loosen, she flashes a smile. That's all it takes for my heart to constrict before twisting painfully in my chest.

POPPY

The knock on the apartment door sends my belly into freefall. I flatten my palm against my lower abdomen, hoping that will settle everything that riots dangerously within. It's as if there's a horde of angry butterflies attempting to wing their way to life inside me.

It's ridiculous how nervous I am about this date. It's not like I haven't been on dozens of them throughout the years. But for some reason, going out with Mason feels like a big deal. I have the sneaking suspicion it's because I like him.

Really like him.

Once I reach the tiny entryway, I inhale one last deep breath before grabbing the handle and yanking the door open. I find Mason standing on the other side of the threshold in the hallway. He's wearing a navy polo and dark wash jeans. Normally, in class, he wears T-shirts. Once, at the garage, I found him bare chested. I'd be lying through my teeth if I didn't admit that I prefer him without a shirt, but he looks seriously handsome dressed like this.

"Hi." That's all it takes for the butterflies to explode for a second time.

"Hey." Heat sparks in his eyes as his gaze skims down the length of me. "You look beautiful."

My hand smooths over the sundress that ends around mid-thigh. I can't help but remember the night he found me stranded along the side of the road. It was the first time he kissed me. My tongue darts out to moisten my lips, almost as if I can still taste him there.

"Thank you." What's funny is that this man has already seen me naked—twice—and yet, I feel nervous and shy around him. Going out on a date shouldn't be a big deal.

But it is.

Our gazes cling for a long moment. It wouldn't take much for me to drown in his dark depths. They remind me of still waters. It's only when you're wading through them that you realize how deep they run.

He clears his throat. "You ready to go?"

"Yup. Let me grab my purse." I swipe it off the small table in the entryway.

Mason steps aside as I walk into the hallway, locking the apartment door behind me. Tension crackles in the air as we head to the stairwell and then the lobby. His truck is parked out front of the building. I'm intensely aware of his bigger body beside me as he holds open the door to the pickup and I slide inside. A handful of seconds later, we're pulling out of the lot.

He flicks a glance in my direction. "I hope you don't mind if we go to O'Donnell's."

I shake my head. It's an Irish pub located on the outskirts of town. They have the best burgers and homemade chips. Not to mention corned beef and cabbage eggrolls.

Yum.

I slant a look in his direction to gage his reaction. "Didn't want to take me someplace close to campus, huh?"

Guilt flickers across his expression. "I figured the fewer people who saw us out together—at least for the time being—the better off we'd be. Are you still good with that?"

Reaching out, I lay my hand over his larger one before giving it a squeeze. "I'm just teasing. I understand why we're not sticking close to Claremont, and it's fine."

His muscles loosen. "I still don't think your father will like this."

"And I still don't think it'll be a problem. If we decide to move forward, then we'll tell him and see who's right."

He huffs out a reluctant chuckle. "I guess we will."

"For the record," I say with more confidence than I'm feeling, "I think it'll be me."

There's a moment of silence before he murmurs, "I hope you're right."

Me, too.

My father has always had a soft spot for Mason, but I have no idea how he'll feel about his only daughter dating an older man.

He slips his hand from beneath mine. Just as I mourn the loss of contact, he drops it over my smaller one. My pulse skitters as I stare at our clasped hands. There's something about the rough callouses marring his palm that sends a shiver dancing down my spine. Mason has the hands of a man who uses them for a living. Not a college boy or someone who sits behind a desk in an office forty or fifty hours a week.

It's beyond sexy.

It takes ten minutes for us to reach the restaurant and another five before we're shown to a table. I glance around, not recognizing anyone who looks to be my age. As we walk through the dining area, I can tell that Mason is also scoping out the situation, although he's more covert about it.

As soon as we're seated, a waitress stops by. He asks for whatever beer is on tap, and I order a glass of water. I see the exact moment the difference in our ages forces its way into his brain again.

"I forgot you're not twenty-one yet," he mutters, brows pinching together.

"Even if I were, I'd prefer water. I'm not much of a drinker."

As soon as the waitress drops off our beverages, he lifts the glass to his lips and downs nearly half the golden liquid.

During the ride over, energy had snapped and crackled between us. Now, the atmosphere feels different. Awkward. Uncomfortable. If it continues, it'll end up smothering whatever is attempting to flourish, and I don't want that to happen.

Needing to get us back on track again, I say, "Did you realize that Anne is ten years younger than my father?"

The corners of his lips wilt. "That's different. They're much older."

"True, but at some point, I'll be older too, and it won't be such a big deal." I lean forward, closing as much distance between us as the table will allow. "You're the only one who thinks it's a problem."

"You're wrong about that."

After the waitress takes our order—burgers and homemade chips for both of us—another silence descends.

"How long have they been married?"

"Almost ten years." I add in case he doesn't know, "My mother died of breast cancer when I was eight."

Emotion flickers in his eyes. "I'm sorry."

"It happened a long time ago, and for the most part, I've made my peace with it."

"Both of my parents are gone, too," he admits. The way he forces out the words makes me think they're not easy to convey.

I nod. "Dad mentioned it."

He shifts on his chair and glances away. "It's been seven years. Sometimes, I can't believe it's been that long, and then other times, it feels like they've been gone forever, and I can barely remember when it was the four of us."

The emotion seeping its way into his deep voice has my chest constricting. Not wanting him to feel so alone, I reach across the table and lay my hand over his. It feels good to offer solace and connect on a deeper, more meaningful level. Most people are so uncomfortable with the idea of death. They give you half-ass platitudes before quickly changing the subject and moving on to a more pleasant topic of conversation.

When he remains silent, I say, "Losing Mom was difficult. I can't imagine what it would have been like to lose both my parents at the same time."

The muscles in his throat constrict as he swallows. "It was hard. My life was totally upended. I had to drop out of school and get a full-time job in order to take care of my younger brother."

I have to fight every instinct to rush around the table and pull him into my arms. My heart shatters for how quickly the man sitting across from me was forced into adulthood. That's too much responsibility for any twenty-year-old to deal with.

"Wasn't there family who could help? Grandparents, aunts, or uncles?"

He shakes his head. "Not really. And they all lived out of state."

"Are you and your brother close?" How could they not be, after suffering something so tragic?

Hunter Price was a senior on campus when I was a freshman. Dad always talked about what a talented football player he was.

Emotion flickers across his face before it's quickly shuttered away. It's only after a few beats of silence that I wonder if he'll answer the question.

"We were for a long time."

His words are so low that I have to strain to hear them.

My brow furrows. "But you aren't anymore?"

"It's complicated."

"Oh." As tempting as it is to dig deeper, it's obvious from his forced responses that Mason doesn't want to talk about the rift in their relationship.

He picks up his glass and takes another drink before setting it down again. "We had a falling out during his senior year of college, and for a long time, we didn't speak."

"I'm so sorry." How much more can this guy deal with on top of everything else?

"Me, too. What happened was my fault. I thought I was making the right decision. Turns out I didn't."

"We all make mistakes."

A steady breath escapes from him. "Yeah, well…this one was huge. And it wasn't something he could get over or forgive." There's a pause before he admits, "I pushed his girlfriend into leaving town so he could focus on his future. They were apart for three years before he found out what happened. Needless to say, he was pissed." His lips reluctantly quirk at the corners. "Actually, furious is more like it."

I dredge my memory, trying to recall bits and pieces of information I've heard over the years regarding Hunter. "Isn't he married?"

"Yup."

When he doesn't elaborate, I ask the question that sits poised on the tip of my tongue. "Is it to the same girl you pushed away?"

"Yeah. Her name is Skye, and they got hitched after graduation."

"Wow. I'm glad they found their way back to one another."

He's silent for a long moment before admitting, "Me too. They belong together."

"That's what matters in the end, isn't it? Finding your person and doing whatever it takes to be together?"

His dark gaze locks on mine, pinning me in place. "I suppose it is."

His low words send an electrical current zipping through my veins, and I get the feeling we're no longer talking about Hunter and his wife.

We're talking about something else altogether.

We're talking about us.

MASON

If I'd been secretly holding out hope that dinner would be a complete bust, that turns out not to be the case. For the most part, there weren't any awkward lulls in conversation. We flowed easily from one topic to another. I hadn't realized that Poppy lost her mother when she was so young. Maybe the circumstances are different, but the loss of any parent is something you don't just get over or move on from.

It's a painful ache that lives in your heart forever.

What is it about this girl that puts me instantly at ease? As much as I want to deny the truth, I can't.

I like her.

A lot.

It occurs to me as we head back to town that I'm nowhere near ready for this night to be over. I don't want to say goodbye and drive back to the loneliness of my place. That's all it takes to make a split-second decision and turn the truck onto a dark country road. She glances at me but doesn't ask where we're going or what I'm doing. We don't know each other well, and she certainly has no reason to trust me, but it's kind of nice that she does.

We drive over a rutted dirt road for about a mile or so before arriving at an open field. This place isn't far from my house, and after my parents died, when I needed to be alone, this is where I always ended up.

It's the first time I've brought someone else with me.

Including Hunter.

After the accident, when it felt like I'd lose it, I would raise my fists toward the heavens and yell out all the grief and heartache that filled me, nearly swallowing me whole. It never changed anything, but I felt better afterward. More at peace. It was the only way to relieve the anguish that was eating me alive. I sure as shit couldn't do it in front of Hunter.

For whatever reason, bringing Poppy here feels right.

I park the truck in the grass and exit the vehicle. She does the same as I grab a thick blanket from the backseat and walk around to the tailgate before lowering it. Then, I jump onto the bed and spread out the blanket. When I'm finished, I find her standing near the rear, watching me with a curious gaze. I extend a hand and help her onto the bed before we stretch out. It takes a handful of seconds to find a comfortable position.

"It's pretty here," she says.

"Quiet too, which is why I like it."

We fall into a comfortable silence as the sky continues to darken and the stars brighten until they resemble pinpricks of light scattered across a velvety canvas. There's something about the vast stretch overhead that calms my inner turmoil. Maybe it's the knowledge that the universe is infinite and when it comes down to it, we're tiny and insignificant in comparison.

She turns her head until her penetrating gaze can settle on mine. This is the first time I've ever felt so emotionally attuned to another human being. I don't understand how that's possible when we don't really know each other, but there's no denying the truth.

I've spent years trying to deaden everything inside me, never wanting anyone to get too close. I didn't have the time or inclination to get involved with a woman. But that's not how I feel about her. At every turn, Poppy is proving to be different.

It's as disconcerting as it is exhilarating.

As much as I want to force her away, the urge to pull her closer and hang on for dear life with both hands is stronger. My chest constricts as these thoughts run rampant through my brain.

Unable to meet her searching gaze, I stare at the sky. When I remain quiet, she rolls toward me until her body can brush against mine. It's so tempting to wrap my arms around her and haul her close. Instead, I remain still, allowing her to make the first move. It doesn't take long. Not more than a handful of seconds pass before she reaches out and runs the tip of her finger across my parted lips.

"I haven't been able to stop thinking about you."

A steady stream of air escapes from my lungs. "Same."

She's been a constant, unwanted presence dominating my thoughts. Even when I didn't want her to be.

Especially when I didn't want her to be.

Her index finger continues to sweep back and forth. When it ventures inside my mouth, I bite down on the tip. It's not hard, just enough to get her attention.

A gasp escapes from her.

That's all it takes for my restraint to snap and my hand to snake around the back of her head, drawing her close enough for our lips to collide. As soon as they do, she opens, and my tongue delves inside her mouth. The sweet taste of her floods my senses.

How will I ever get my fill of this girl?

Instead of dwelling on that thought, I shove it from my brain and focus on how good she feels in my arms. She fits perfectly. Almost as if she were made for me. Or maybe it's the other way around. I have no idea.

What I do know is that when we're together, I feel complete. Life hasn't felt that way for a long time.

One hand slides from the nape of her neck to her hip as the other fastens onto the opposite side so I can hoist her on top of me. Her legs part as she straddles my pelvis. The soft material of her dress falls around us and her panty-covered pussy gets nestled against my rock-solid length. I've been fighting a boner for most of the night, and I can't do it any longer.

I flex my hips, rolling them against her. My hands tighten to hold her in place as her head tips, exposing the delicate column of her throat.

God, but she's beautiful. Especially against the backdrop of the night sky. I don't think I've ever felt more at peace than I do at this moment.

"Mmmm…that feels so good," she whispers.

The only thing better than this is being buried deep inside the heat of her body.

I told myself before picking her up that our date wouldn't end with sex. We'd talk. Get to know each other.

"Poppy…" My fingers bite into her flesh.

She lifts her head to meet my heavy-lidded gaze. "What?"

"We shouldn't take this any further."

"Why not?" Leaning forward, her fingers pull at my polo, forcing it upward until it's gathered around my chest. Her palms sweep over the bare flesh as her gaze tracks each movement. "We want each other." She slants a look at me. "Don't we?"

"Yes."

"Then I don't see what the problem is."

I release a steady breath as her fingertips brush over my nipples before lazily circling them. All of my resistance crumbles. Especially when her hands drift to my belt buckle. She hesitates as her questioning gaze meets mine. Somehow, our roles have flipped and now she's the one seeking out permission to take things further.

Maybe I was a fool to believe that tonight would end any other way than this.

When I jerk my head into a nod, she loosens the buckle before flicking open the button and lowering the zipper. She scoots back just enough for her fingers to slip inside my boxers and wrap around my cock. A groan slides from my lips as I thrust into her palm.

Fuck me, that feels good.

I don't understand how everything she does makes me feel like I'm going to come undone. It doesn't make a damn bit of sense. She's a twenty-year-old girl. I've been with a shit ton of women, ones who knew how to suck the chrome off a bumper, and I still managed to control myself. All this one has to do is wrap her hand around my dick and I'm ready to blow my load.

Ridiculous.

"Do you have a condom?" she asks, breaking into the intense pleasure crashing around inside my brain. Which is probably for the best. A few more pumps and I'd likely embarrass myself.

"Back pocket, in my wallet."

One hand stays wrapped around me while the other slips to the pocket of my jeans. She grabs the wallet before setting it on my chest.

"I could get it, but then I'd have to—"

"I'll get it," I blurt.

Her lips tremble as she strokes my length. "I figured that might be your answer."

I flip open the wallet and grab the condom before tossing the leather aside. As I tear into the package, ready to cover my cock with latex, she reaches for the foil square.

"Let me do it."

I blink at the unexpected offer.

When I hesitate, she holds out her hand and I lay the thin square in her palm. Carefully, she pulls out the rubber before yanking down the elastic band of my boxers until my erection can spring free. My heartbeat picks up its tempo when she scoots further down my thighs and leans down to run the tip of her tongue over my cock. Back and forth she strokes as I fight to keep the groan trapped inside. When she sucks the crown into her mouth, that becomes impossible.

Holy fuck.

"Poppy," I mutter, precariously close to losing it.

This is exactly what she does to me. No matter how many times I try to convince myself that she's no different from any other woman, she continues to blow that theory to shit. When her suction turns voracious, I thread my fingers through her long, blonde hair. I'm not sure if I'm trying to keep her in place or rip her away.

"There won't be a need for that condom if you keep it up much longer." And when I say much longer, I'm talking minutes.

Possibly seconds.

She releases me with a soft pop before pressing a kiss against the tip. And then she's carefully rolling the latex over my length. Have I ever been this hard? Or so close to losing it when I wasn't even inside a woman?

Nope.

Never.

Once my dick is covered, she shifts, spreading her legs further apart before stretching her panties to the side and positioning her body over mine. My gaze settles on her bare pussy and my mouth waters for a taste. It's been way too long.

I hiss out a breath when she lowers herself onto my shaft, taking me one inch at a time until I'm completely buried inside her body.

As good as the blowjob felt, it's nothing compared to this.

I allow Poppy to set the pace and take control of the situation. Her palms settle on my chest as she flexes her hips. It doesn't take long for us to find a rhythm. This is the first time we've had sex that isn't frenzied, and there's something nice about it.

I'm so damned turned on that I have to grit my teeth in order to keep a firm grasp on my self-control. I'll be damned it I come before she does. Her head rolls back as she continues to move on top of me.

My gaze goes from the place we're intimately connected to the expression on her face, and I'm once again bowled over by how beautiful she is with the breeze wafting through her blonde strands and the silvery moonlight spilling over her.

When her pussy spasms and a whimper escapes from her lips, I finally allow myself to lose control, diving headfirst over the cliff with her.

I glance at the text from Dad before pushing into the locker room and winding my way through the space. My footsteps echo off the cinderblock walls as I head to the back where the offices are located. Practice doesn't start for another hour, so the place is more like a ghost town than football central with guys in various states of undress.

When I reach the open door, I poke my head into the small room crammed with old tapes, playbooks, photographs, and trophies, only to find it empty. Dad said he'd be here, watching game film. With a frown, I glance at my watch. I have ten minutes before I need to hustle to my next class.

Just as I'm about to fire off a text, a deep voice says, "Sneaking into the guys' locker room again, huh?"

Startled, I swing around, and find Mason. As soon as our gazes collide, his lips quirk at the corners.

My hand flies to my chest as my heart thunders a painful beat. "You scared the crap out of me!"

A chuckle escapes from him as he flashes a grin. "I must have. You nearly jumped a foot."

I blink.

Have I ever seen Mason laugh? Or tease? Or smile like that?

I don't think so.

Broody Mason is attractive, but playful Mason?

He's even more so.

It wouldn't take much to fall hard for him.

"What are you doing here?" he asks, cutting into my thoughts.

I hold up my phone as evidence, just in case he really thinks I'm sneaking in here to get an eyeful. Honestly, he's the only eyeful I want. "I was looking for Dad. He asked me to stop by, but he's not here."

"One of the trainers wanted to talk with him. He should be back any minute."

I glance carefully around the empty space to make sure we're alone before stepping closer and twining my arms around his neck. When I lift onto the tips of my toes, his arms snake around my ribcage to press me closer.

"We shouldn't be doing this here," he groans. "Someone could walk in and see us."

"Practice doesn't start for an hour," I whisper.

Before he can argue, I nip at his lower lip, tugging it with my teeth. A growl escapes from him as his mouth crashes onto mine and our tongues tangle.

This is how I like Mason best.

When his mind clicks off and he allows himself to live in the moment.

As the kiss deepens, the world shrinks down until it only encompasses the two of us. Wrapped up in his arms with our bodies perfectly aligned, I feel the steely length of his erection dig into my belly. It's so tempting to—

"Wow. Guess this would be the reason you wanted me to stay away from her. Huh, Coach?"

Startled by the deep voice that echoes off the walls, we splinter apart as a gasp falls from my lips and we stare at Levi.

Not once does the football player glance in my direction as he continues to glare at the older man.

Before Mason can offer an explanation, the QB turns on his heel and stalks away. The heavy metal door opens before getting slammed shut again as I stare at the last place I saw him standing before disappearing around the corner.

"Fuck," he mutters, dragging a hand through his short, dark hair.

My fingers sweep across my lips, which already feel swollen from his kisses. "I'm sorry." In hindsight, making out in the locker room was reckless.

He glances at me, and the tension filling his shoulders dissolves. "It's not your fault. I knew better, and should have put a stop to it before it got out of hand."

Even though what happened doesn't feel like a good thing, maybe it is. Maybe now, we can stop sneaking around.

"You know," I say cautiously, "if we tell Dad that we're seeing each other, then there won't be a reason for us to hide our relationship."

"Is that what this is?" He jerks a brow. "A relationship?"

Uncertainty rushes through me. Is it possible that I've read too much into this? "I thought so."

Just as the muscles in my belly contract, a smirk flashes across his face as his hand snakes out to nab my fingers before drawing me closer. "You know it is."

He presses a kiss against my lips.

"I was hoping to give it a little more time before we told your father. Maybe if I talk to Levi, he'll keep quiet about what he saw."

It takes effort to swallow down my disappointment. Doesn't he understand that life would be so much easier if we were out in the open and didn't have to worry about people catching us? I totally get that he doesn't want to jeopardize his new job, but I honestly don't think Dad would fire him.

"Okay. Sure."

When the locker room door swings open again, Mason takes a few hasty steps in retreat until there's at least four feet of space to separate us.

"Hey, sweetheart," Dad's voice booms as he strides around the corner. By his easy expression, I can only assume he didn't run into

Levi in the corridor. "Sorry about that. I thought it would be a quick five-minute conversation with the trainer. Turned into twenty."

"It's not a problem."

He stuffs his hands into the pockets of his shorts. "Have you been waiting long?"

"Nope. Just got here."

He glances at Mason before jerking a thumb in the younger man's direction. "Hopefully this guy kept you company."

The way his lips were crushed against mine minutes ago flits through my head.

I clear my throat along with those distracting thoughts and keep my attention focused on Dad. "Yeah. We were talking about your schedule for the season."

With a nod, he glances at his assistant coach. "Anne was just saying this morning that dinner with the four of us worked out so well, we should find the time to do it again."

The words sit perched on the tip of my tongue. It wouldn't take much to push out the truth and let the chips fall. One glance at the tension radiating from Mason is enough to swallow them back down again.

What's clear from our conversation is that he's not ready for us to go public.

My biggest fear is that he never will be.

POPPY

With an extra fifteen minutes before the start of class, I decide to stop by the coffee house on campus and pick up an iced latte. I need something to get my blood pumping, and with any luck, this will do the trick.

If not, I'm in for a long morning.

As I open the door, I realize quite a few people had the same idea. I step into the queue and wait patiently for my turn.

Thankfully, the baristas are used to the heavy student traffic and keep the line moving at a steady clip. As another person steps up to the counter and places their order, a voice from behind says, "Hey, Poppy."

My heart stutters as I glance over my shoulder and find Levi. We haven't spoken since he walked in on Mason and me kissing in the locker room. I caught sight of him in class a couple days later. Instead of parking himself next to me like usual, he sat with a couple of friends. When he refused to meet my gaze, I'd assumed he was angry.

"Hi." My fingers flutter nervously before tucking a stray lock of hair behind my ear. "How are you?" I steel myself, unsure if I'm about to get an earful.

"I'm good." He glances at the large picture window that takes up most of the front wall. "Looks like it's gonna be another nice one today."

When he flashes a smile, I blink, surprised by his friendly demeanor. Whatever I was expecting, this wasn't it. He doesn't seem angry at all.

Is it possible I had it wrong and he never had feelings for me?

I release a steady stream of air as my muscles loosen in relief.

But still…

I feel like I should apologize for what he walked in on and make sure we're good. More importantly, I don't want him mentioning it to my father. Or anyone else. The last thing we need is rumors flying around campus.

"About the other day…I'm sorry if you were thrown off by what you saw." I clear my throat as heat stings my cheeks. "I'd thought we were alone."

He hikes a brow. "In the guys' locker room? Seems like an awfully strange place to make out, but whatever floats your boat."

I glance around, hoping no one overheard his comment.

"You're right. It shouldn't have happened," I mutter. I can't deny that part of me wants to go up in flames.

Like I need Levi's judgment?

I don't think so.

"How long have you two been seeing each other?"

"Not long," I admit. "We're still pretty new."

"Does Coach know?"

My teeth sink into my lower lip as I give my head a quick shake.

"Huh." His hand rises to scratch his chin as he shifts his weight. "I can't imagine him being happy about it."

Everything inside me stills. "Why would you say that?"

"Seriously?" Disbelief flashes across his expression. "Because the dude is like…thirty-five or something."

"He's twenty-seven," I correct, irritated by the direction this convo has swerved in.

"Same difference," he says with a careless shrug.

"Not really." Twenty-seven is hardly old.

"You're like, twenty—a junior in college—and he coaches with your dad. Isn't it kind of weird that you're dating one of your father's friends?"

"They're not friends," I mumble.

Not really.

The dinner invitation from the other day pops into my head. All right...so maybe they're kind of friends.

Levi's face scrunches. "Do you think Coach will fire him when he finds out you two have been sneaking around behind his back?"

Fire him?

My mouth turns cottony at the thought, and it takes effort to force the words through stiff lips. "Of course not. Why would he do that?"

"I don't know. He might not be cool with his assistant coach hooking up with his daughter. Plus, won't it be awkward when you two break up?"

"We've barely started to date," I point out.

The corners of his lips quirk. "Come on, Pop...do you really think something between you two will last for the long haul? Like you're gonna get married, have babies, and all that stuff? Can you actually see that happening?"

"I don't know," I whisper. It's way too early to mentally trip down that path.

"Maybe you need to give this relationship a little more thought before breaking the news to your old man. Once you let that cat out of the bag, there's no putting it back in again, and I'd hate to see Coach Price lose his job. All the guys on the team really like him."

There's no way Dad would fire Mason...right?

The thought makes me nauseous.

When I remain silent, Levi jerks his head toward the counter. "Looks like it's your turn."

I blink out of the stupor that's fallen over me. "Umm, thanks."

"Sure. No problem." He points toward the door. "I need to take off, but I'll catch you later."

By the time I lift my hand in a wave, he's already gone, pushing out into the sunshine.

Our conversation swirls through my head as I order the latte I no longer want. Whenever I've broached the subject about talking to my father, I've been adamant that he would be fine with us dating.

It's only now that doubts crop up within me.

The last thing I want is for Mason to lose his job.

His dream job.

Because of me.

And I certainly don't want to cause a rift in his relationship with my father. Especially now that I'm aware of the issues with Hunter.

How is it that I'd felt so certain about our path forward thirty short minutes ago and now…

Now I'm none too sure.

MASON

From the corner of my eye, I watch Poppy as she lounges on the counter in the garage as I work under the hood of a Ford Mustang GT. The carburetor has been running a little rough, and I'm hoping that if I give it a good cleaning, it'll take care of the problem. If not, the old one will need to be replaced.

Instead of concentrating on the car, I glance at the girl who forced her way into my life. I can't go more than a few minutes without her normally smiling face popping into my head.

She's been unusually quiet since walking through the door almost an hour ago.

Now that I think about it, she's been preoccupied for the past couple of days. I'm not sure what it means.

Maybe nothing.

Maybe something.

It's the *maybe something* that concerns me.

Even though alt rock plays in the background, her silence feels deafening. I've tried several times to start up a conversation.

Each one has stalled.

Normally, the girl is a veritable chatterbox. Talking about her day before asking how mine went. It might not be something I have a lot of experience with, but I like it.

Unwilling to let this stillness linger, I set the wrench down on the engine and swing around to face her. It's almost a surprise to find that she's not paying attention to me.

That's a first.

Her brow is furrowed as her gaze stays locked on her sandals.

"Poppy?"

Her head jerks up at the sound of my voice. "Yeah?"

It only takes five strides to swallow up the distance between us. The closer I get, the further she has to tip her head in order to hold my searching gaze.

My hands settle on her cheeks, the thumbs gently stroking over her lush lower lip. "You've been awfully quiet this afternoon. What's going on?"

If I'd thought I was jumping the gun or my assessment of the situation was off, the guilt that flickers across her face tells me that's not the case. When she breaks eye contact, my fingers tighten around her chin, redirecting her gaze back to me.

I want to know what's eating her up inside.

More like I need to know.

"Talk to me, baby. I have no idea what's going on inside your head."

The reluctance in her blue depths is what scares me most. Poppy might not realize it, but her face is so expressive, and she wears her emotions for all to see. It's one of the things I like about her. From our first run-in, I knew what she was thinking. The desire was evident in her expression.

I always want her looking at me that way.

With longing and lust.

And someday...love.

"I don't think we should see each other anymore," she whispers, shattering the thoughts inside my head and scattering them to the wind.

I blink as the air evaporates from my lungs until it feels like I can't breathe.

"Oh."

That's all I've got.

My brain spins on an endless loop as I stand rooted in place and stare in shock, hoping that somehow, I've misunderstood the words that just tumbled from her lips.

"I'm sorry."

Sorry.

Sorry for crashing into your life and making you feel things you never expected or wanted to feel in the first place.

Maybe I shouldn't be surprised by this sudden twist.

Poppy is young.

She's entitled to change her mind.

Just because she's the best thing that's ever happened to me, doesn't mean it's the same for her.

It takes effort to fight down the riotous emotion gurgling up inside me, fighting to break free and spew everywhere. "Why?"

Her gaze flickers away before returning of its own accord. "You were right about us being in different places."

I was right...

There's not much I can say to that. She was so insistent this could work, and I was desperate to believe her.

Believe this had a fighting chance to flourish into something more.

It's the reason I was against getting involved in the first place. She's a junior in college and a full-time student. Her life is stretched out in front of her. She should be going to parties, football games, and dating guys like Levi.

But that's not where I am.

Barely can I remember a time when I didn't have the weight of the world resting on my shoulders, crushing me to the earth.

There's absolutely nothing for me to say.

"Okay." My hands fall away from her face, drifting uselessly to my sides.

The crystal-like tears pooling in her eyes turn them luminous. All I want to do is drag her to me.

But I can't.

I won't force or guilt anyone into loving me.

When she remains still, I say gruffly, "You should go."

With a jerk of her head, she sucks in a deep breath before sliding off the counter. Even though I've retreated, she closes the distance before reaching out and cradling my cheek with her palm. I can't help but press my face into her soft touch.

When her tongue darts out to moisten her lips, I shake my head, forcing out the command. "Go."

There's only so much I can take.

She blinks as a single tear treks down her cheek. "I'm sorry, Mason."

I lock my muscles so I won't fall to my knees and beg her to reconsider. "There's nothing for you to apologize for. We gave it a shot, and it didn't work out. No harm, no foul."

It would be so much easier if I believed those words.

If they were the truth.

She reaches onto the tips of her toes and presses a kiss against my lips before drawing away and searching my eyes one last time. "Goodbye."

"Bye."

With that, she walks away.

Out of my garage.

And my life.

POPPY

"Give me your honest opinion." Anne holds up a pale pink blouse at the boutique we've spent the last twenty minutes browsing in. "What do you think of this?"

She sent a text the other day, asking if I'd like to do a little shopping and then grab lunch. Since my classes are all scheduled in the morning, I agreed. She's a district attorney for the county, and every so often, she likes to play hooky.

Anne came into my life when I was ten years old and still mourning the loss of my mother. She was married and lost her husband to colon cancer a year before Mom died. They met in a support group and struck up a friendship before it eventually turned into something more. I'm glad Dad is married again, and that Anne is the woman in his life. I wouldn't want him to be alone.

And neither would Mom.

"It's really cute." I consider the silky top for a few seconds. "It'll look nice paired with your light gray suit."

She flashes a smile before sending me a wink. "My thoughts exactly. See? Great minds really do think alike."

I snort and continue perusing the racks for anything that jumps out at me. So far, Anne has fallen in love with a couple different pieces, but I haven't found anything that grabs my attention.

If I'm being perfectly honest, I'm not really in the mood to shop. Even though it's been a couple of days, I can't stop dwelling on Mason and how blindsided he'd been after I blurted out that we should break up. Hurt and disbelief flashed across his face before being shuttered behind a stoic mask. It had taken every ounce of self-control not to break down and tell him the truth. He probably thinks I'm the world's biggest flake and is kicking himself for ever getting involved with me.

I can't blame him for that.

What he doesn't realize is that I inflicted just as much pain onto myself when I hurt him. There was no other way around it. The more Levi's comments circled through my head, the more sense it made to pull the plug.

Shoving out the words had been one of the hardest things I've ever had to do.

"It seems like something's bothering you," Anne says, drawing my attention back to her.

I glance up from the shirts I'm pretending to inspect and meet her inquisitive stare. "No, I'm fine."

She studies me with more care from across the rack. "Really? Because it doesn't seem like you're fine. I couldn't help but think the other night when you were over for dinner that something was going on. I didn't want to pry, so I let it go, but it's been a couple days and you still seem like you're in a funk." There's a pause before she adds in a gentle tone, "I'm concerned. Even your father mentioned it after you took off."

My shoulders collapse under the heavy weight of her words. "Is that why you suggested shopping and lunch this afternoon?"

She flashes a lopsided smile. "A little retail therapy never hurt anyone."

I huff out a reluctant chuckle. I suppose she's right about that.

"But mostly, I was hoping we could talk. You know I'm always here if you need me."

"I do. And I appreciate it." Honestly, it means everything to me.

When I remain silent, she quips, "If you don't tell me, I'll be forced to use my superior cross-examination tactics on you."

I chew my lower lip before mumbling, "It's nothing."

"Ahhh, so it is, indeed, *something*."

"I guess." When she pops a perfectly manicured brow, I grudgingly admit, "I was seeing a guy, but we decided it would be best to break it off."

She blinks in surprise. "I didn't realize you were going out with someone."

Guilt suffuses me. "We wanted to keep it under wraps until we were sure it would lead to something more." I force my shoulders into a shrug. "See? There wasn't much point to saying anything, because it's already over."

"What happened? Why did it end?"

There's zero point in telling her that the man in question was Mason. When it comes down to it, I have no idea how she or my father would react. I might have told Mason that Dad wouldn't have a problem with our relationship, but I have no idea if that's the case.

I think me dating an older guy would have been a shock in the beginning, but they would have come to terms with it.

Eventually.

While my father has always been protective, as I've gotten older, he's allowed me the freedom to make my own decisions. Just like he allows me to feel the full weight of the consequences from those choices. He's never been one to swoop in without allowing me to first work out the problems for myself.

"It's complicated." That seems like the easiest response.

"Hmmm," she says with a nod. "Relationships can be challenging."

"Yeah."

"But sometimes we make them unnecessarily difficult when they don't have to be."

I shake my head, wishing that were the case. "No, this one is definitely sticky. As much as I wish it didn't have to be, there isn't a way around it. At least for the time being. I don't know…maybe in the future, that'll change."

"Well, that's a shame."

"It is. I really liked him," I admit. None of the guys I've dated in the past have affected me this way. They never came close to making my heart pound or my panties dampen the way Mason did.

"Perhaps the situation is worth revisiting to see if it can be salvaged." She allows those words to sink in before adding, "Relationships aren't easy, but finding someone you get along with and feel connected to is rare. And it shouldn't be discarded simply because it takes work."

My teeth sink into my lower lip before chewing on it. "I don't know."

Mason has suffered enough heartache and pain. The last thing I want to do is inflict more damage.

It's so tempting to come clean. To get everything out in the open and see what her reaction is. It's highly doubtful she'd be doling out encouraging advice if she knew the truth.

But being honest would put Mason at risk, and I'm unwilling to do that.

MASON

"The team's really shaping up," Coach says, standing next to me on the sidelines with a clipboard in hand. "Moving Erickson to the O line was the right decision."

I nod in agreement. "He's comfortable there and will make more of an impact."

"Yup." He yanks off his ballcap before wiping the sweat from his brow. "It's hot as Hades out here."

I glance at the cloudless sky. He's not joking. Even though it's the middle of September, temperatures are still hovering in the eighties. On the turf, it feels even hotter. Some of these boys aren't from the South. They're not used to this kind of heat and humidity.

"I have to say that you joining the program midway through the summer has gone smoother than expected."

"It's been a great experience so far," I tell him.

"How are your classes? I know you were worried about them giving you trouble. Is that still a concern?"

"Nope, they're going well." Which is a surprise. I fully expected to crash and burn. "There was a bit of a learning curve in the beginning but I'm getting the hang of it."

He nods, looking pleased with the admission. "I knew you would. In a couple years, you'll have a degree to hang on the wall."

It's definitely one of the perks to working at the university.

When I remain silent, he adds, "And the guys have really taken to you."

"They're a good bunch." For the most part. There are always a couple boneheads who need a little extra guidance, but that goes with the territory. Just the other week, a freshman player was picked up by campus police at two o'clock in the morning for underage intoxication. On top of the ticket, he's now benched for three weeks and needs to complete a mandatory substance abuse program with the university.

"Is there anything on your mind that you'd like to discuss?"

I glance at him, surprised by the question. "Nope." In fact, this coaching gig couldn't be going any better.

Shifting his stance, he continues to stare at the players scrimmaging on the field. "Denison," he barks, "where the hell are you supposed to be?"

The kid freezes.

"Wrong!" He points to a different place on the field. "Hustle over there."

There's a pause as the kid gets into position.

"Better."

Silence descends as we watch the play unfold.

Just when I think he's dropped the previous conversation, he says, "The reason I ask is because you've seemed a little off lately." He squints against the sun. "I was worried you might be having second thoughts about coming on board."

Instead of admitting the truth, I say, "No second thoughts. I'm good."

As good as I can be, considering that the girl I was falling for just smashed my heart to smithereens.

"Guess there must be something in the air, because Poppy doesn't seem much like herself these days either."

My gaze slices to him. "Oh?" The last thing I want to do is appear overeager to hear about his daughter, even though that's exactly what I am. "Is something going on?"

He shrugs as his gaze stays focused on the field. "Not really sure. She was over for dinner last week and just didn't seem like her normal bubbly self." He flicks a glance in my direction. "For the most part, she's always been a happy kid."

It takes everything I have inside not to wince.

Kid.

Because that's exactly what she is.

"Her mother's death was a difficult time for her." His expression softens. "You'd understand that better than anyone."

"Yeah." It's just one of the things we have in common.

"She and Anne grabbed lunch and did a little shopping the other day. My wife was hoping Poppy would open up and tell her what's going on."

My chest constricts as every muscle becomes whipcord tight. "And did she?"

"A little." Coach frowns. "Guess she just went through a breakup."

"Oh." Everything inside me plummets.

"No father wants to see his little girl get her heart broken."

I smash my lips together to stop myself from blurting out the truth. "Why do you think it was her heart that got broken?"

"From everything she told Anne, she cared a lot for this guy."

"She still could have been the one who pulled the plug and walked away." If I'm smart, I'll shut down this conversation before it can spiral any further out of control.

His expression turns thoughtful. "Whatever happened, I think there were a lot of feelings involved." His gaze slices to mine before searching it. "You know what I mean?"

I'm not sure.

Maybe?

If I'd thought moving on from Poppy would be easy, I was wrong. She's always there in the back of my head.

I've spent more time than I'm comfortable admitting with my phone in hand, trying to screw up the courage to reach out.

But how can I do that when she's the one who called it quits?

Plus, all the obstacles that were standing in our way are still there. They haven't magically disappeared.

So...there doesn't seem to be much point calling or texting.

Except to twist the knife a little deeper.

Here's a little bit of irony I try not to dwell on—over the years, there have been countless women who have issued ultimatums. When they didn't get what they wanted, they walked away. Their disappearance from my life never bothered me. Not really. There might have been a momentary flicker of regret, but after a few days, it disappeared, and I moved on.

That hasn't been the case this time.

"I'm sure she'll get over him," I say gruffly. Forcing out those words is painful. I don't want her getting over me, and I sure as shit don't know when I'll be able to do the same.

"I don't know. I've never seen her like this."

"It'll just take time."

"I suppose that's possible. From everything she told Anne, the situation was complicated."

When I remain silent, he continues, "Tell me when life isn't complicated."

Unable to do so, I grunt in agreement.

Whether he's meant it or not, the wheels in my head have begun to turn. It's the last thing I need. Or want. If Coach knew I was the guy his daughter was seeing, he'd be fucking furious.

And probably feel betrayed.

I certainly can't blame him for that.

Over the years, Coach has been good to my family. He took me under his wing when I came into his program as a player, and even when I dropped out of college, he made sure to stay in touch. I could always count on his phone calls.

When Hunter signed with Claremont, Coach made sure he was awarded a full ride to the university. There's no way we could have afforded a college education if not for that. And now, my brother is playing in the pros.

So…I owe this guy big time.

The last thing I want to do is hurt him or his family.

That's not how you repay someone who's always been there for you.

When a heavy hand lands on my shoulder, I snap back to the conversation. "I need to head back to the office and make a few calls. I should be gone for about twenty minutes or so. Think you can handle everything out here?"

"Yeah, sure. No worries."

He smiles. "I know there aren't any. Like I said before, I'm glad you're part of the program."

"Me, too," I say honestly.

"You know, I don't dole out a lot of unsolicited advice, but I'm going to give you my two cents, since you're more like a son to me."

"Shoot." I force down the thick lump that has settled in the middle of my throat. Over the years, Derek has become important in my life. Someone I can go to for advice. Pleasure bursts inside me, knowing that the feelings are reciprocated.

"Nothing about these past seven years has been easy. You took on more responsibility than any twenty-year-old kid should've had to." When I open my mouth to protest, he shakes his head and cuts me off. "I realize there wasn't a choice in the matter, but you still did it. For years, you put your brother first and didn't think about yourself. Not many people would have been willing to make those tough decisions. The fact that Hunter is living out his dreams is a direct result of your sacrifices." He searches my eyes. "You get that, right?"

I jerk my head into a nod as my chest constricts.

"Now that your brother is gone, it's time for you to focus on yourself for a change and figure out what makes you happy. I'd like to think this job is a good start."

I clear my throat and try to keep all the emotion fighting to break free in check. "It has been."

"I'm glad to hear that. If I have my way, you'll take over this program when I retire."

I've been so overwhelmed with school and everything that goes along with learning the ropes of a new position that I haven't given much thought to where this job could lead in the future. I'm just trying to take life one day at a time.

"I—"

"You don't have to say anything. We're talking sometime down the road," he adds with a chuckle. "But that's what I'm thinking."

"Thank you. The confidence you've placed in me means a lot."

"There's nothing to thank me for. What I want is for you to start thinking about yourself and your dreams. Maybe that includes finding someone to share your life with."

With another clap on my back, he takes off for the tunnel that leads to the locker rooms. I blow out a steady breath as everything he just said ricochets around in my brain.

"Your dad is planning to fire up the grill when he gets home," Anne calls out from the kitchen where she's preparing a few salads to go along with dinner.

"That sounds good," I answer back from the living room where I've been camped out for the past couple of hours doing homework. Even though I have my own place, I've been spending more time here lately. I like being around Anne and Dad. And having the pool in the back-yard is certainly no hardship. Sometimes, it's just nice to stop by, eat a homecooked meal, study for a bit, and then lay out by the water.

I promised myself that I'd study for another hour and enjoy their backyard oasis before heading to my place for the night.

When the doorbell rings, Anne says, "Would you mind answering that?"

"Sure." I jump off the couch and pad to the door before yanking the handle.

My eyes widen when I find Mason standing on the porch with his hands stuffed inside the pockets of his khaki shorts. "Hi."

"Hey." His solemn gaze pierces mine and I find myself straining forward, trying to get closer before realizing what I'm doing.

When he says nothing more, I drop my voice. "What are you doing here?"

Is it possible Dad invited him over for dinner? Didn't he mention that when the three of us were together?

"I was hoping we could talk." Before I can ask how he knew where to find me, he admits, "I stopped by your apartment and your roommate said you were here."

A flurry of nerves explodes in the pit of my belly as I tuck a stray lock of hair behind my ear. "What did you want to talk about?"

"Us."

My heart skips a painful beat. "Us?"

"Yeah." He steps closer as I hug the door. "I know we weren't seeing each other for long, but I'm not ready for whatever this is to be over."

"Mason—"

"No. Hear me out. I like you. More than I've ever liked another woman, if I'm being perfectly honest."

Air rushes from my lungs as I admit, "I like you, too."

The admittance throws him off guard and his brow furrows as confusion flickers in his dark eyes. "If that's the case, then why did you break up with me?"

I glance away before gnawing my lower lip.

"Poppy," he growls. "Look at me."

My gaze slices to his. "I didn't want to see you lose anything more than you already have."

"I don't understand," he says slowly as if I'm not making a damn bit of sense. "How would I lose anything else?"

"Your job. School." I take a hesitant step closer. "I didn't want to see either of those things taken away from you. Especially since I know how much you enjoy coaching."

"I guess this is my fault. I wanted to give our relationship a little more time to develop before we told other people. But that was a mistake. All it did was allow doubts to creep inside your head. I think the first thing we need to do is talk to your parents."

I scrape my teeth across my lower lip. The last thing I want is for him to feel pressured into going public. "Are you sure?"

"Yeah, I am."

His hand snakes out to nab my fingers. Before I'm able to suck in a full breath, he pulls me closer, and I find myself locked tight against the solid strength of his chest. "You know what I've discovered in the time we've spent apart?"

When I shake my head, he says, "That you're more important than anything else."

"How can you say that when we haven't been together very long?"

His warm breath feathers across my lips. "Because it feels like forever since anything has felt right in my life, but with you, it does. What we've found is special, and I don't want to let that go. I don't want to let *you* go." He searches my eyes. "I need to know you feel the same and that this isn't all one sided."

"I do. I feel it, too."

As soon as the words escape, his lips crash onto mine. That's all it takes for me to open so our tongues can tangle. Relief sweeps through me as my arms twine around his neck. If I have my way, I'll never let him go.

It's only when someone clears their throat from behind me that we jump apart. Still wrapped up in Mason's arms, I swing around to find Dad and Anne standing in the living room. My father raises a brow and Mason pulls me even closer, as if he's afraid they might try to steal me away.

"Dad," I say nervously. I've introduced a number of guys to my family, but none of them have mattered the way Mason does. Even though this relationship is new, I need them to be okay with it.

"Is there something you'd like to tell us?" Dad asks, a serious expression marring his face.

I straighten my shoulders and inch my chin upward before digging deep to find my courage. "Mason and I have been seeing each other."

Dad glances at his assistant coach. "Can I assume this is the guy you broke up with because the situation was," he raises his fingers before making air quotes, "*complicated.*"

My gaze flickers to Anne.

"Sorry, sweetie. He was worried about you."

I huff out a breath. Maybe I should be mad at her for sharing our private conversation with my father, but I'm not. Above all else, I know she had my best interests in mind.

"Yes, it is."

He cocks his head. "What exactly made it complicated?"

I blink.

That's not the question I was expecting.

"Well…Mason is seven years older than me." There's a pause before I tack on, "He's also your assistant coach."

"Both of those things are certainly true," Dad says carefully.

"And I didn't want him to get fired."

"Fired?" His eyes widen as his brows snap together. "Why would anyone fire Mason?"

"I—"

Both his voice and expression soften. "You have to know I'd never do that, honey. Mason is a great coach, just like I knew he would be. And if I have my way, he'll take over the Clairemont program at some point in the future."

"Really?" My mouth falls open, and it takes a second or two for my brain to start working again. "So…you don't mind if we date?"

"Mason is a good man." He smirks at the younger guy who continues to stand with his arms wrapped protectively around my body. "You could do a hell of a lot worse than him."

The rush of relief that whips through me is enough to weaken my knees.

Now that we're all on the same page, Anne takes hold of my father's hand. "How about you start the grill and these two can talk in private." She glances at Mason. "I assume you'll be staying for dinner?"

"Yes, ma'am."

"Then I'll set the table for four," she says with a smile before they walk out of the room holding hands.

Once we're alone again, I turn in Mason's arms until I can meet his dark gaze.

"I've missed you this past week," I admit, looping my arms around his neck and pressing close. Why does everything feel so much better when we're together?

His lips brush mine. "I missed you, too. I wish you would have just talked to me about your concerns and how you were feeling. We could have avoided all of this."

That was my mistake. I allowed Levi to get inside my head. Even though it's tempting to tell him what happened and explain the full story, I keep it to myself. There's no point in stirring up hard feelings when it's his job to work with the QB.

"You're right, I should have been honest. I'm sorry."

He nips at my lip, tugging it with his teeth as our gazes cling. "Just as long as you're mine now."

"I am, Mason. I'm yours."

EPILOGUE

MASON

*wo years later...*

MY HEAD IS STUCK **under** the hood of a cherry red 1967 Dodge Charger. She's a real beauty.

Even though I've been coaching for a couple of years now, I still enjoy getting my hands dirty when time allows, which isn't often, but I enjoy working on American muscle. It's what I specialize in as a side hustle. When we're in the middle of the season, time is limited, and I'll only take on one vehicle a month.

It keeps me busy and out of trouble.

From beneath the hood, I hear her footsteps over the alt rock that plays in the background and fills the cavernous space.

"Hey, babe," I call out, always happy when she wanders out to the pole barn to keep me company.

"Hey, yourself."

The fridge door opens before closing again. "I thought you could use a beer. You've been out here working for a couple hours."

I straighten to my full height and stretch my aching muscles. "Thanks. Seems about that time, doesn't it?"

"Sure does."

My eyes eat her up as she closes the distance between us. She's barefoot and wearing another flirty sundress that does amazing things for her lush curves. When there's no more than a foot or so to separate us, she hands over the bottle.

I've said it before, and I'll say it again—there's something sexy about a barefoot woman wearing a sundress.

It gets me going every damn time.

Maybe I should amend that statement—there's something about my woman walking around barefoot while wearing a pretty sundress that gets me every single time.

"You look good enough to eat," I tell her.

A sly grin flashes across her face. "That was the idea."

Before I can ask what she means, her fingers pluck the ties at her shoulders. A second later, the soft material floats down her body before puddling at her feet, leaving her completely bare.

When I continue to stare, she slowly backs up until her ass hits the counter. With her palms braced on the linoleum, she hoists herself on top of it. Her gaze stays locked on mine.

"Fuck," I growl.

"I was hoping for that, too," she says with a smirk.

I stalk toward her before setting the bottle on the counter. The beer, which I'd been so thirsty for a minute ago, is now completely forgotten.

I'm more interested in my fiancée. The one who lives with me. The one who crashed into my life—literally—and turned everything upside down and inside out. The very same one who I'll marry after she finishes her master's degree in education.

I cage her in with my arms, pushing her backward until my chest is pressed against her naked breasts and my lips can hover over hers. I'm so damn hungry for the taste of her. It's always like this between us.

Hot.

Explosive.

Cataclysmic.

When Poppy is in the room, I'm blind to everyone else. It didn't take long for her to become my entire world.

Without further prompting, she opens her mouth so our tongues can tangle. The whimper that escapes from her only heightens the need crashing around inside me. My cock throbs with painful awareness as one hand snakes between us to loosen my belt, flicking open the button and lowering the zipper in one swift motion. I grip the boxers, yanking them down until my erection can spring free. All I can think about is how good it'll feel to sink inside the heat of her body.

One thrust of my hips and that's exactly where I am. A groan rumbles up from within my chest as I bury myself balls deep in her softness.

Every time I do, I take a second—just one—to glory in the sensation. Being inside this girl feels very much like being home. It's something that was lacking from my life for a long time.

But I found it again in her.

Poppy is my home.

No matter what happens in our lives, she'll always be my home.

And that's not something that will ever change.

***

Have you read Hunter & Skye's story? Turn the page for a sneak peek!
You can check out Heartless here -)
https://books2read.com/u/m2Moq7

Read the Heartless prequel for free -) https://bookhip.com/
RZSTWWG

HEARTLESS

SKYE

"Yay! The bitches are back together again, and tonight we ride!" Lanie wraps her arms around me and squeezes tight. "It's been too long, girl! *Way too long!*"

A reluctant smile curves my lips. "I know. It's good to be back." The circumstances surrounding my return are less than ideal, but I'm happy to see Lanie again. She's been my best friend since middle school, and I've missed her. FaceTime and texting are nice, but it's not the same as talking in person. She links her arm through mine as we walk across the open field.

I glance at the cute cowboy boots that adorn her feet. When she told me that we were going to a field in the middle of nowhere, I didn't believe her.

That was my first mistake.

Second mistake?

Not going with sturdier footwear.

Instead, I'm wearing a pair of flimsy sandals. They're cute as hell, but that's not going to do me a whole lot of good across this terrain.

Lanie insisted we celebrate my return by dragging me to a bonfire in a farmer's field. Already, the place is crawling with drunk-off-their-asses, barely legal adults. Shouting and raucous laughter fill the balmy night air.

Even though I know it won't do me any good, my gaze coasts anxiously over the ever-swelling crowd. Nerves dance across my spine as I silently pray Hunter will be absent from the revelry. Or, if he is here, we'll somehow be able to avoid one another.

If I know Lanie—and I do—she'll be up my ass to cut loose and have fun. How can I do that when Hunter and I now attend the same college? At any given moment, I could turn a corner and smack right into him.

The thought of that happening makes me nauseous.

As much as I want to play it cool and act like my ex-boyfriend doesn't matter, the words slip from my mouth before I can stop them. "You don't think he'll be here, do you?" I shoot her a look that's rife with concern.

Lanie doesn't bother to ask who I'm referring to. She doesn't have to. She's all too aware of my past. She had a front row seat to our relationship and its demise.

"I don't know." She pauses and pops her shoulders into a careless shrug. "Maybe."

"What?" My feet grind to a halt as my mouth dries, turning cottony. I'm barely aware of the blades of straw poking my feet through the leather sandals. "But you said—"

Her expression hardens, transforming into one of impatience. "Even if he *is* here, the chances of you running into him are slim." She waves an arm toward the massive group of students who have gathered to mourn the end of summer by drinking themselves into a stupor. "Look around. Half the university is here. There's no way you're going to see him, Skye, so stop worrying about it and live a little."

My teeth sink into my lower lip before I suck the fullness into my mouth. No matter what Lanie says, I'm going to worry.

When I remain silent, my best friend plants her hands on her hips and glares. Here comes Lanie's version of tough love.

"Would you rather sit home by yourself on a Saturday night

because you're too chickenshit to show your face? Afraid that you *might* run into Hunter Price?"

I'm sorry, is that really a question?

From the annoyed expression that flickers across Lanie's face, I decide to keep those thoughts to myself.

"Skye Elizabeth Sinclair!"

I wince as my full name cracks through the air. It brings an unpleasant image of my mother to mind. This is what I get for living with someone who isn't afraid to call me out on my bullshit. Maybe I should have taken Dad up on the offer to live with him.

I decide to go with something close to the truth. "I was hoping to avoid him for a while," I mutter. "That's all."

And when I say a while, *what I really mean is forever.*

Is that really too much to ask?

Lanie sighs as her expression softens. Marginally. "I know, but you're going to run into him on campus or at a party eventually. It's inevitable. Accept it and move on."

I snort.

Easy for her to say. Lanie doesn't have any ghosts from her past that are ready to jump out and scare her.

I have a carefully constructed plan in place for the year. It involves lying low and flying under the radar, so Hunter doesn't even know I'm here. "Yeah, I guess…"

Unwilling to let me backslide, Lanie loops her arm through mine and pulls me toward the growing group of partiers. "It'll be fine. I promise."

Unfortunately, my bestie isn't in a position to guarantee me anything, and we both know it.

The closer we get to the party, the more my anxiety ratchets up. At least night has fallen. The only light emanates from the bonfire that flickers in the distance and the stars that twinkle across the dark velvety sky.

For the time being, I'll remain vigilant. There's really nothing more I can do.

I inhale a deep breath before carefully blowing it out.

Maybe Lanie's right, and I'm making a big deal out of nothing. It's been three years since we've seen each other, and a lot has happened since then. We've both moved on with our lives. I'm sure he's forgotten all about me. As those thoughts circle through my head, my shoulders loosen from around my ears, and my heart stops thumping a painful beat.

The moment we reach the outer ring of people, Lanie is swept off her booted feet and spun around in a tight circle like a rag doll. Her short floral dress flies around her thighs. Laughter rings throughout the air as her arms slip around her boyfriend's neck.

Jaxon Conway has a typical football player's physique. He's a mountain of a man—tall, broad in the shoulders, and muscular. He looks like he could easily bench press Lanie's VW Bug. I would be intimidated by him, but he's quick to laugh and has warm brown eyes. He's like a teddy bear—big and gruff on the outside but tender and mushy on the inside.

"Missed you, babe," he growls.

"It's only been a couple of hours since we saw each other!"

"Doesn't matter," Jax complains. "I still missed the hell out of you."

"Aww." Lanie's voice softens, becoming dreamy. "I love you so much."

"I love you more," he responds with enough heat to melt the panties off Lanie's body.

Ugh.

Make it stop.

These two are so sickeningly sweet that I get a toothache every time I'm around them. Although, if anyone deserves a good guy, it's Lanie. Like most girls in their early twenties, she's dated her fair share of assholes. Jaxon is almost too good to be true. Kind of like a mythical unicorn that sprang to life. He's an athlete who isn't interested in screwing as many girls as he can get his hands on.

Ever since I rolled into town a few days ago, Jaxon and Lanie have been glued together at the hip. I get the feeling he'll be our unofficial third roommate for the year.

Know what's been getting a lot of use?

My noise-canceling headphones.

Most nights, those two sound like they're auditioning for a porno. Let's hope it calms down soon.

Jaxon and Lanie coo at each other before their mouths fuse, and they start going at it like a pair of cats in heat. I clear my throat and glance everywhere but at them. If we were hanging out at the townhouse, this would be my cue to exit stage left. But we're not at home; we're in the middle of a field a few miles from town. There's nowhere for me to go, and no one for me to talk to.

Awkwardness descends as I flick a piece of straw from my shirt.

Maybe I should take this opportunity to grab a beer. There must be a keg around here somewhere. You can't have this many college kids congregating in one spot and not have alcohol. That would be considered sacrilegious, right?

With any luck, by the time I return, Jaxon and Lanie will have stopped mauling each other long enough for us to move on with our evening. It's not like he's being shipped off to war tomorrow and they'll never see each other again.

Sheesh.

My gaze meanders to them in hopes that they've gotten their fill of each other.

Nope. The face sucking has become even more intense. Any moment, clothing is going to spontaneously combust from their bodies.

I don't really want to be around when that happens.

So…a beer it is.

Not that either of them is paying me the least bit of attention, but I point toward the mass of bodies that have multiplied in the fifteen minutes since we've arrived. "I'm going to grab a drink." When my words are met with kissy noises, I say, "Try not to miss me too much while I'm gone."

Lanie waves a hand absently in my direction as they continue to get it on.

"Okay then," I mumble before reluctantly taking off on my own.

The number of people gathered here is a little overwhelming.

Lanie's right; half the university must have shown up. Everyone is talking, laughing, and drinking. In other words, they're having a great time.

Me, not so much.

It takes a good ten minutes to find the keg. Or maybe I should say *kegs* since there are six of them next to the back end of a midnight black pickup truck blasting music from massive speakers. I can barely hear myself think over the thumping bass. Then again, maybe that's for the best. It's a relief to get out of my head, even for a few minutes.

I locate the line for the beer and take my place at the end of it. I'm not much of a drinker, but I need something to smooth out all of the rough edges so I can relax and enjoy myself.

My flesh prickles with awareness, and I run my hands over my arms to banish the disconcerting sensation. I glance around, scouring the crowd for one face in particular but don't see him anywhere. That alone should alleviate my anxiety, but it doesn't.

My parting with Hunter wasn't what one would call amicable. I don't blame him for being hurt and angry. Whether Hunter understands it or not, I did what needed to be done. As painful as it was, I'd do it all over again. I loved Hunter more than life itself.

A part of me still does.

Probably always will.

If everything I've read online is true, then my sacrifices have been well worth it. Hunter will get snapped up in the NFL draft before graduating this spring. Ever since I can remember, that's been his goal. If one person deserves for all his dreams to come true, it's Hunter Price. Unwilling to dwell on my ex, I shove him from my mind and take in the scene before me.

People are gathered together in groups, greeting one another as if they're long-lost friends who haven't seen each other in decades. It's surreal to be surrounded by so many people yet feel so removed from it all. As if I'm more of an observer than a participant. Other than Lanie and Jaxon, I don't know anyone else. I'm sure people from high school attend CU, but I lost touch with most of them after I moved away.

By the time I make it to the front of the line, I'm antsy and ready to head back to my friends. Even if they're still going at it. Which is really saying something. I'd much rather stand around as a third wheel than be an island onto myself. I dig through my front pocket and hand over a couple of bucks in exchange for a blue plastic cup before it's filled to the rim with golden liquid.

The cute guy manning the keg flashes me an easy grin as his eyes drift over my body. When he's finished with his perusal, his gaze once again settles on my face. Kudos to this guy for not gawking at my boobs like he's never seen a pair of D cups before.

"Here you go, beautiful," he says, handing over the cup with a gallant flourish.

This little bit of silliness lightens my mood. "Thanks."

Our fingers brush as I take the Solo cup from him.

"Next time, cut to the front of the line." He gives me a flirty wink. "I got you covered."

I flash him a grateful smile. Maybe tonight won't be so bad after all.

With my drink in hand, I'm ready to make my way back to Jaxon and Lanie. Only now does it occur to me that they could have moved from the spot where I'd left them.

Who's to say I'll even be able to find my way back?

A knot of unease settles at the bottom of my belly. My fingers go to the purse slung across my chest. It's big enough to hold my phone, but that's about it. I could always shoot Lanie a text, but who knows if she'd hear it. And I have no idea how to navigate my way back to our apartment. The unsettled feeling that had taken up residence in my gut turns into full-on nausea.

Only now do I realize that walking away was a bad idea. I should have stuck to Lanie and Jax like glue. But standing around and watching them make out felt pervy.

And not in a good way.

With those thoughts swirling through my brain, I spin around and slam into a wall of impenetrable muscle. The impact knocks me off-balance, and I stumble back a step. Before I can fall, strong hands reach out and grab my shoulders, yanking me forward. My breath catches, and my heart pounds at the narrowly avoided tumble.

I shake my head to clear it as beer sloshes over the rim of my plastic cup and spills onto the ground at my feet. I'm lucky it didn't end up down the front of my top or the shirt of the unsuspecting person I plowed into.

How humiliating would that have been?

Ugh...I don't even want to think about it.

"I'm so—"

My voice falls off as I glance up, my gaze colliding with narrowed blue eyes. Hunter quickly sets me free as if his fingers have been burned. Neither of us breaks eye contact. All of the raucous noise of the bonfire dies away until it's just the two of us standing alone in the middle of a dark field.

This is the moment I've been dreading.

My eyes roam over his face, cataloging the myriad of changes that time has wrought. When I walked away, Hunter had still been a boy, his lean muscles beginning to thicken. Now the transformation has been complete, and he's a full-grown man. Hunter has always had size on his side, but somehow, he's managed to grow both taller and broader. He must be somewhere in the vicinity of six three or four. I have to crane my neck to hold his gaze. The graphic T-shirt he's wearing stretches tautly across the wide expanse of his chest and hugs the chiseled strength of his biceps. It's enough to make my mouth dry and my knees soft.

If I have one weakness, it's for thickly corded arms. All that tightly harnessed power waiting to break free...

A shiver of desire scampers down my spine before I stomp it out.

Unaware of the effect he's having on me, Hunter's deep voice cuts through my thoughts.

"What are you doing here, Skye?"

It's the harshness of his tone that has my gaze snapping back to his as heat floods my cheeks. I can't stop myself from staring. The little bit of cyberstalking I've done over the years has in no way prepared me for coming face-to-face with my ex-boyfriend. He's grown into his dark looks, becoming even more of a heartbreaker than he was in high school.

My tongue darts out to smudge my parched lips as nerves dance along my skin. I search Hunter's eyes, looking for any hint of softening, but there's none to be found. His gaze is as frigid and detached as I imagined it would be. The tiny kernel of hope that our time apart would be enough to heal our past wounds shrivels and dies inside me.

There is no forgiveness in his heart.

But then again, did I really expect there would be?

Maybe. It would have made coexisting on campus for the next year so much easier.

It's obvious from his terse behavior that Hunter would prefer to pretend I never existed in the first place. As much as I would love to give him that, I can't. Unforeseen circumstances have forced me home.

I straighten my shoulders and attempt to keep my voice level. I don't want him to hear the slight tremble that is working its way through my body. "I transferred to Claremont for my senior year."

His shadowed jaw ticks as he clenches his teeth. *"Why?"*

The way he bites out that one word leaves me wincing.

I take a quick step back and lift my chin, not wanting him to see how much power he still holds over me. Time has done nothing to diminish it. "That's none of your business."

Whether Hunter realizes it or not, he still owns a piece of my heart. It's better for both of us if he never suspects the depth of my feelings.

His hands tighten into fists as he closes the little bit of distance that I've managed to put between us. Instead of scrambling back the way every instinct is clamoring for me to do, I hold my ground until we're standing toe-to-toe. My heart pounds a painful staccato against my breast as his harsh breath feathers across my parted lips.

There was a time when I couldn't get close enough to Hunter.

Now I can't get far enough away.

Sorrow floods through every fiber of my body that it has to be this way between us. Next to Lanie, Hunter was my best friend. He was my first everything.

Date.

Kiss.

Love.

Heartbreak.

Everything we once shared has been blown to pieces, and we're nothing more than strangers. Actually, what we are is much worse. His animosity is palpable. It radiates from him in suffocating waves that threaten to choke the life out of me.

"You shouldn't have come back," he growls. "You don't belong here anymore."

That may be true, but there's nothing I can do about it. I'm here. And I'm not going anywhere.

I shift my weight and force myself to say, "Claremont is big enough for the two of us."

"No, it's not. Stay the fuck out of my way, Skye." His eyes flash with barely suppressed hostility. "You won't like the consequences if you don't."

Before I can summon up a retort, he stalks away. Rooted in place, I track his movements until he fades into the crowd. Not once does he turn around and acknowledge my presence. I've been dismissed. Relegated to the black hole that is our past.

Once he disappears from sight, my knees weaken as the pent-up breath rushes from my aching lungs.

I haven't been on campus for a full seventy-two hours, and in Hunter's eyes, I'm public enemy number one.

Want to read more of Skye and Hunter's story?
Check out Heartless here -) https://books2read.com/u/m2Moq7

CAMPUS PLAYER

DEMI

"*M*orning, Demi!" Gary, one of the stadium custodians, calls out with an easy smile and wave as he saunters toward me. "Up and at 'em bright and early this morning, I see."

My heart jackhammers beneath my ribcage from the twenty-minute run as I flash him a grin. "Always!"

"You have a good one! I'll see you tomorrow!"

Since I've already moved past him, I holler over my shoulder, "Same place, same time!"

Even with *The Killers* pumping through my earbuds, I almost hear the deep chuckle that slides from his lips. Our morning greetings are a ritual three years in the making. I've been running through the wide corridor that leads to the stadium football field since I stepped foot on campus freshman year. This will be something I miss when I graduate in the spring. Five days a week, I'm up at six, logging in a four-mile run before returning home, jumping in the shower, and heading off to class.

At this time of the day, the stadium is still relatively quiet, with only a few people wandering the hallways. There's something both serene and eerie about it. I've been here on game days when there are thirty thousand fans packed shoulder to shoulder, rooting on the

Western Wildcats football team. Three-fourths of the stadium filled with black and orange is an amazing sight to behold. Football is a religion at Western. Unfortunately, the same can't be said for the women's soccer team. We're lucky if there are a couple of hundred spectators in the stands.

I've come to terms with it.

Sort of.

I keep my gaze trained on the light at the end of the tunnel and push myself faster. As soon as I burst out of the darkness, bright sunlight pours down on me, stroking over the bare skin of my arms and shoulders. It's late August, and summer is still in full swing. A whistle cuts through the silence of the stadium, and my gaze slices to the field. Nick Richards has been head coach of the Wildcats for the last decade. He also happens to be my father.

Two days a week, the guys are up at six in the morning for yoga. Dad is a big believer in flexibility. Even though I'm winded, a smirk lifts the corners of my lips. Watching two-hundred-and-eighty-pound linebackers contort their bodies into Downward-Facing Dog, the Warrior II Pose, and the Cobra is enough to bring a chuckle to my lips. Some of the guys actually like it, but most grumble when they think Dad isn't paying attention. Little do they know that he sees and hears everything.

My father catches sight of me and flashes a quick smile along with a wave in my direction. He has a black ball cap pulled low and aviators covering his eyes. There's a clipboard in one hand as he paces behind the instructor.

When I point to the field, he shakes his head. He might make the guys do yoga, but he refuses to participate. Something about old dogs and new tricks. Every once in a while, I'll tell him that he needs to get out there and set a good example for the team. He usually shoots me a glare in return.

Every Wednesday night, Dad and I get together. Our weekly dinners became a thing when I moved out of the house and into the dorms freshman year. He's busy coaching football, and my schedule is packed tight with school and soccer. Getting together once a week is the best way for us to stay connected. It doesn't matter if we're in the middle of our seasons; we always make time for each other. Especially since Mom lives in sunny California. After eighteen years of marriage, she got fed up with being a distant second to the Western University football program. She packed up her bags and walked out. I hate to say it, but Dad didn't notice her absence for a couple of days. Which only proved her point. Now she's remarried, learning to surf, and is a vegan. I visit for a couple of weeks during the summer before soccer training camp starts up at the end of June.

Even though it's only the two of us, our weekly dinners are set for three people.

I tell myself to stare straight ahead and not glance in his direction.

Don't do it!

Don't you dare do it!

Damn.

My gaze reluctantly zeros in on him like a heat-seeking missile. Long blond hair, bright blue eyes, sun-kissed skin, and muscles for miles. And he's tall, somewhere around six foot three.

I'm describing none other than Rowan Michaels.

Otherwise known as the bane of my existence.

My dad discovered the talented quarterback the summer before we entered high school and took him under his wing. Which has been...aggravating. In the seven years since, Rowan has become an irritatingly permanent fixture in my life. He's the brother I never wanted or asked for. He's the gift I wish I could give back. He's the son my father never had but secretly longed for.

On a campus with over thirty thousand students, one would think that avoidance would be easy to accomplish. That hasn't turned out to be the case. Somehow, we ended up in the same major—Exercise Science. I get stuck in at least one class with the guy each semester. This time it's statistics, which is a requirement. Three times a week, I'm forced to see him. And then there are the weekly dinners at Dad's house.

Every Wednesday, Rowan shows up without fail.

It's so annoying.

No, *he's* annoying!

Our gazes collide, and electricity sizzles through my veins before I immediately snuff it out and pretend it never happened.

I am not attracted to Rowan Michaels.

I am not attracted to Rowan Michaels.

I am not attracted to Rowan Michaels.

Maybe if I repeat the mantra enough times, it'll be true. That's the hope I cling to. I've made it through the last seven years trying to convince myself of this. I only have to get through our final year together, and then we'll go our separate ways—me to graduate school or maybe to the Women's National Soccer League, and Rowan to the NFL. He's one of the most talented quarterbacks in the conference. Hell, probably the country. There is little doubt in my mind that he'll be a first-round draft pick come next spring.

Trust me when I say that Rowan Michaels fever is alive and well at Western University. His fanbase is legendary. The guy is a major player.

Both on and off the field.

Girls fall all over themselves to be with him. They fill the stands at football practice, show up at parties he's rumored to be at, and basically stalk him around campus.

It's a little nauseating. Don't these girls have any self-respect when it comes to a hot guy?

I wince at that unchecked thought.

Fine...I'll begrudgingly admit it; he's good-looking.

I shake my head as if that will banish the insidious thoughts currently invading my brain. Enough about Rowan. It's time to focus on the reason I'm at the stadium at this ungodly hour. I rip my gaze from him as I hit the cement staircase. After half a flight, all thoughts of the blond quarterback vanish from my mind. How could they not when my quads, glutes, and calves are on fire, screaming for mercy as I force myself to the nosebleed section. By the time I finish, my legs are Jell-O, and I still have a two-mile run back to the apartment I share with my best friend off-campus.

I give Dad a half-hearted wave before leaving. It's the most I can muster. His lips quirk at the corners as he shakes his head. He thinks I'm crazy. At the moment, I can't argue with his assessment of the situation. Although, it's the extra training I put in that helps me run circles around the other team in the second half of the game.

The jog home feels like it will last forever. By the time I unlock the apartment door, I'm ready to collapse. I beeline for the shower and jump in before it's fully warm. My skin prickles with goose flesh, but it feels so damn good. Twenty minutes later, I'm dressed and ready to take on the day. My hair has been thrown up in a messy bun, and I'm making a protein smoothie that will fuel me for my morning classes.

Just before taking off, I poke my head into Sydney's room. I know exactly how I'll find her, and that's buried beneath a small mountain of blankets. She doesn't disappoint. We met the summer before freshman year in training camp and have been besties ever since. She's the yin to my yang. The peanut butter to my jelly. The Thelma to my Louise. Where I'm more introverted and cautious, she's loud and boisterous. She's been known to leap without necessarily looking at what she's jumping into. Every so often, it gets us into trouble. Sydney and I have lived together since sophomore year. I gave up trying to cajole her ass out of bed for a six o'clock run after the first week of us cohabitating when she nearly took my head off with an alarm clock.

"It's that time again," I sing-song obnoxiously, "rise and shine."

There's a grunt and then some shifting from under the blankets that tells me she's alive.

When I chant her name repeatedly, each time escalating in volume, she growls, "Get the fuck out!"

"Awww," I mock, "that's so sweet. I love you, too."

Sydney snorts before a hand snakes out from beneath the blankets to give me a one-fingered salute. Then she grabs a pillow and tosses it in my general vicinity. It falls about five feet short of its mark.

I stare at the dismal attempt. "If you're trying to cause bodily harm, you'll have to do better than that."

"Piss off."

"All right then." I shrug. "See you after class." With that, I close the door behind me.

My farewell is met with another indecipherable mouthful. If this weren't something we went through on the daily, I'd worry she was in the midst of a stroke. Sydney is definitely not a morning person. She's more of an early afternoon person. Another thing I've learned over the years? The action of waking up to a brand-new day is a gradual process. She's like a bear rousing prematurely from hibernation. It's not a pretty sight. She's lucky I don't take her insults personally.

I grab my backpack from the small table crammed into the breakfast nook area along with a coffee before heading out the door. The apartment I share with Sydney is located three blocks from campus, which is highly sought out real estate. We're fortunate Dad is friends with the guy who manages the building. It's probably one of the only perks of having a father who is a head coach of a college football team.

You'd think there would be more, but you'd be wrong. Honestly, being Nick Richard's daughter is more of a hindrance than anything else. People assume you receive special treatment on campus, from professors, or that you have an in with all the football players.

Or worse...

Much worse.

After a bunch of ugly—not to mention untrue—rumors circulated freshman year, I've done my best to distance myself from the Wildcats football team. They're a great bunch of guys, but I don't need all the ugly gossip and speculation that comes along with being friends with them.

As I reach Corbin Hall, the mathematics building for my stats class, my gaze is drawn to a clump of students standing around outside the three-story, red-brick building. In the center of that crowd is Rowan. I don't have to see him physically to know that he's close. The muscles in my belly contract with awareness. It's like a sixth sense. One I wish would go away. He's the last person I want to be cognizant of.

As I jog up the wide stone stairs to the entrance, my gaze fastens on him. A smirk twists the edges of his lips, and my eyes narrow before I drag them away and yank open the door to the building.

Relief rushes through me as I step inside the air conditioning and disappear from sight.

"Hey, Demi, wait up!"

I turn at the sound of my name before slowing my step. The dark-haired guy jogging to catch up smiles before falling in line with me.

Justin Fischer.

He's a baseball player and teammates with Sydney's boyfriend, Ethan. We've been seeing each other for about a month. It's still casual at this point. With school and soccer, I don't have a ton of time to invest in a relationship. He seems to understand that and isn't pushing to be more serious.

When he leans in for a kiss, I angle my head. At the last moment, he tilts in the opposite direction, and we end up bumping teeth instead of locking lips. With a grunt, I pull away and chuckle. My fingers fly to my mouth to make sure I haven't chipped a tooth.

Maybe I've been reluctant to admit it to myself, but that kiss sums up our relationship perfectly.

Awkward and a step out of sync with each other.

"Sorry," he murmurs with a slight smile. I search his face and wait for any telltale sign of sexual chemistry to ping inside me. Unfortunately, my insides remain completely unfazed, which is disappointing but not altogether unexpected. I had a sneaking suspicion when we first got together that it might turn out this way.

"No problem," I say, hoisting my smile and brushing aside those thoughts.

"I haven't seen you for a couple of days," he remarks as we turn a corner and continue walking.

"It's been busy." Which isn't a lie. School might have recently started, but the academics at Western are rigorous. And being a Division I athlete is more like a job. If you're not ready to put in the work, don't bother showing up. There's no half-assing it around this place.

"When's your next game?" he asks.

"Tomorrow at six." My gaze flickers in his direction. Not that I expect him to come, but...

Fine, so maybe I do. If he wants to be my boyfriend, then he needs to show a little support.

His dark brows draw together. "That sucks. I've got a mandatory study hour I have to attend."

I shrug off the disappointment. It's another nail in the coffin of this relationship as far as I'm concerned. "That's cool. It's not a big deal."

"But I'll see you tonight?"

Oh. Right.

Tonight.

Well, damn. In a moment of weakness, I threw out an invitation to join our Wednesday evening dinner. It's one I now regret. If only there were a gracious way to rescind the offer.

"If you're busy, I totally understand—"

"Are you kidding? No way." With a grin, he shakes his head. "I wouldn't miss it for the world. I'm looking forward to meeting Coach Richards."

Great. So this is more about my father than me? Exactly what every girl wants to hear.

I force a brittle smile. "Awesome. He's excited, too."

That might be something of an overstatement.

Justin nods toward the end of the corridor. "I better get moving. Professor Andrews is a real stickler for punctuality."

"Yup. See you later."

This time, when he leans in, our lips align perfectly. The kiss is nothing more than a fleeting caress. There and gone before I can sink into it.

And I'm left feeling...absolutely nothing.

I bury the disappointment where I can't inspect it too closely before giving him a wave as he takes off. For a moment, I stand rooted in the hallway and watch as he disappears through the crowd. There's nothing to distinguish Justin from the thousands of guys who look exactly like him on campus. He's of average height and build with dark hair and espresso-colored eyes. He's nice enough. Although, if I'm completely honest, he's a little self-absorbed. He talks about baseball all the time. If Ethan hadn't introduced us, he's not someone I would have looked twice at. We don't have a ton in common.

As much as I hate to admit it, this relationship has probably reached its expiration date.

Now it's a matter of pulling the plug.

Ugh. I hate breakups. Although, it's doubtful this will end up destroying him. I'll have to make it through tonight and figure out the rest.

With a sigh of resignation, I head to the classroom and find a seat tucked away in the far corner of the small lecture hall. A lanky guy I recognize from a few of my other classes settles beside me. He flashes a dimpled smile as we empty our backpacks.

The tiny hair at the nape of my neck rises seconds before Rowan enters the room. It's like my body knows when he's within a thirty-foot radius. I glance at him from beneath the thick fringe of my lashes before shifting away. Air becomes wedged in my lungs as I wait for him to take a seat. And it won't be next to me because I'm—

"Hey man, would you mind moving?"

Surrounded on both sides.

Damnit. I'm hoping the cutie next to me will tell Rowan to go take a flying leap.

What? It could happen. Not everyone at this university is enamored of the football-playing god. Although I realize the odds aren't stacked in my favor. Rowan is the most recognized athlete on campus. People fall all over themselves to accommodate him.

It's a little sickening.

Okay, maybe more than a little.

"Sure, no problem, Michaels." The guy next to me hastily packs up his books before vacating the desk. Unable to ignore him any longer, I glare as Rowan slides onto the seat next to me.

"Did you really think you could evade me that easily?" Laughter brims in his deep voice. A voice, I might add, that does funny things to my insides.

"One can always hope, right?"

"Oh, answering a question with a question." He leans closer, eating up some of the much-needed distance between us. "I like it."

I roll my eyes as his lips stretch into a satisfied grin. Irritation bubbles up inside me when sexual tension blooms at the bottom of my belly. Or maybe that tension has settled a little lower.

It's definitely lower.

I'm tempted to swear like a sailor. How is it possible that I feel nothing for the guy I'm actually dating, and yet my pulse skitters out of control for someone I don't even like? It's so freaking ironic. It's been this way since we met, and nothing I do stomps it out. I can try to fool myself into believing it's not there, but that doesn't make it any less true.

It's a relief when Professor Peters takes his place at the podium and clears his throat. Once he's captured everyone's attention, he delves headfirst into the probability of dependent and independent events.

Grateful for the excuse to ignore Rowan for the next fifty minutes, I open my textbook and concentrate on the lesson. Just as the blond boy fades into the background, his bare knee bumps into mine. Electricity ricochets through my entire being. I glance at him to see if he's noticed the strange energy we always seem to generate and find his ocean-colored gaze fastened to mine.

My guess is that he does.

Damnation.

Want to read more of Demi & Rowan?
Check out Campus Player here -) https://books2read.com/u/
mYAxqV

ABOUT THE AUTHOR

Jennifer Sucevic is a USA Today bestselling author who has published twenty-three New Adult novels. Her work has been translated into German, Dutch, and Italian. Jen has a bachelor's degree in History and a master's degree in Educational Psychology. Both are from the University of Wisconsin-Milwaukee. She started out her career as a high school counselor. She currently lives in the Midwest with her husband and four kids.

If you would like to receive regular updates regarding new releases, please subscribe to her newsletter here-
Jennifer Sucevic Newsletter (subscribepage.com)

Or contact Jen through email, at her website, or on Facebook.
sucevicjennifer@gmail.com
Want to join her reader group? Do it here -)
J Sucevic's Book Boyfriends | Facebook

Social media links-
https://www.tiktok.com/@jennifersucevicauthor
www.jennifersucevic.com
https://www.instagram.com/jennifersucevicauthor
https://www.facebook.com/jennifer.sucevic
Amazon.com: Jennifer Sucevic: Books, Biography, Blog, Audiobooks, Kindle
Jennifer Sucevic Books - BookBub